THE CHOSEN GUN

So far as Chade Stocker was concerned when Capital City hired his gun, it was just another heat-blasted town down on its luck and in need of a little Colt .45 peace-making. He showed no mercy for any of the outlaw gangs, or the wild women, or the desperadoes they sent to kill him. It was only when young Jesse McKidd rode in to face Stocker down that the county would know which man was indeed the chosen gun.

CHAD HAMMER

THE CHOSEN GUN

Complete and Unabridged

LINFORD
Leicester

First published in Great Britain in 2006 by
Robert Hale Limited
London

First Linford Edition
published 2006
by arrangement with
Robert Hale Limited
London

British Library CIP Data

Hammer, Chad
   The chosen gun.—Large print ed.—
Linford western library
1. Western stories
2. Large type books
I. Title
823.9′2 [F]

ISBN 1–84617–548–8

Published by
F. A. Thorpe (Publishing)
Anstey, Leicestershire

Set by Words & Graphics Ltd.
Anstey, Leicestershire
Printed and bound in Great Britain by
T. J. International Ltd., Padstow, Cornwall

This book is printed on acid-free paper

1

A Gunman Came Riding

Chade Stocker leaned on a broken-down bar in a nowhere town and drank his whiskey straight.

As it did always that time of day when the wind coming in off the desert was whispering and whining against the unpainted walls of Dockerty's Saloon, the whole lopsided structure began to creak and groan like a sinner in torment.

'Nice day,' swag-bellied Dockerty said amiably, running a nervous finger around his shirt collar. Having long plied his trade at his place on the fringes of the Nogales Desert, the saloonman was a hardy old veteran of his trade yet the occasional stranger could still make him nervous.

Stocker had disturbed from the

moment he walked in, boosted through lopsided batwings on a ragged gust whipping in from the west. The fact that the stranger was big and brown-skinned and packed a Peacemaker low on his right hip wasn't enough in itself to spook Dockerty, for this veteran got all kinds here, badmen from the Pecos, wild-eyed hellers from the Capital and gun-hung loners from no place at all.

It was Stocker's silence and steady drinking that caused his unease and sparked his curiosity. For experience had taught that a combination like that could sometimes lead to trouble.

He needn't have worried, for despite his sobering appearance, Chade Stocker didn't represent trouble today, was just stopping off here on his way to someplace else.

His original plan upon reaching the desert regions had been to continue on south-west to stop over at the Hard Luck Trailhouse up on Little Yellow Creek, which was as deep as he'd ever ventured into the vast Nogales Desert and Canyon County previously.

A combination of head wind, a king-sized thirst and the old urge to tie one on before taking on a tough new job had seen him steer his palomino into one-horse Pintada, which was acutely aware of his presence by now.

A man could come to Dockerty's to get drunk, get laid, get into a ruckus and ride out without anybody ever knowing his name.

That set-up appealed to Stocker and he was finding the atmosphere, the liquor and the simple luxury of just kicking back and letting go before heading southward for the County Capital very much to his liking.

Although the drinkers were leaving the big stranger be, thanks to Dockerty most everyone realized they were entertaining Chade Stocker by this.

The reason the saloonman knew the gunman's name was due to the fact that he'd once seen it along with an accompanying photo in a faded yellowing copy of the *Desert Denouncer* beneath a headline that read:

THREE DEAD IN PAWNEE FORK!

About all he recalled of the accompanying article now was that a trio of road agents had died in that famous shootout, and this big somber man had done the shooting.

'Get you somethin' to eat, Mr-er . . . Stocker?'

The response was a slight shake of the head and so Dockerty let him be.

The afternoon wore on and drinkers came and went, some darting apprehensive glances at the bronzed stranger in brown, but most content to down their liquor, puff through a durham or two then get on about their business.

A deep afternoon silence descended over Pintada, a languid quietness which might have continued on into the approaching night but for the arrival of the Dunstans just on dusk.

If the desert town could claim anything approaching an elite, the Dunstan family was it.

Pintada had been a sawmill town before the Civil War, but the cut over hills to the west, the gray mountains of sawdust still visible and the crumbling old mill told how it had begun to die. The war had made a huge demand on the limited supply of good timber hereabouts. The Confederacy had stripped the near hills bare, had taken a final despairing look at the good lumber unavailable across an impossible chasm, then left the town to die.

It survived mainly because of Dockerty's and the turpentine plant. The plant, squat, ugly and sprawling, stood on the west side of town and was responsible for the putrid stink that was as much a permanent part of Pintada as the broken-down saloon. Apart from a handful of trades folk and shopkeepers, the men of Pintada made their living either working in the plant itself, or jerking pine stumps out of the grudging earth from which the turpentine was extracted.

Old Man Dunstan owned the plant and his sons ran it. Their power was absolute and they were by nature suspicious of strangers. After taking one look at the solitary figure down the far end of the bar, the trio, one little old man with eyes like a bull rattler and his two husky boys, turned their back on him and cross-questioned Dockerty. Who was he? What brought him here? Could he be a government man looking into unpaid taxes, maybe?

Indifferent to the interest he was arousing, Stocker could finally feel the whiskey begin to hit. He perched on a stool and took out the makings, big hands swift and sure as he fashioned a quirly.

The drinking session before taking on a gun job had become a ritual over the years. The work was always violent and he had no reason to believe this one might prove any different. He was a gunman by trade and such men who drank on the job usually died young. So he liked to get his drinking over with where it was safe to do so, before signing on. It was just one of his habits for survival in the most dangerous trade of all.

The light began to fade and Dockerty shuffled about lighting his tin-shaded lamps. The Dunstans had finally lost interest in the stranger by the time their attention was diverted by the arrival of the drummer. The brothers' eyes lit up. He was a trim little fellow in neat suit and four-in-hand tie. He had travelling salesman written all over him, but old Dunstan's boys saw him immediately as a diversion. He was little, obviously alone and just as plainly nervous in a place where only the rugged survived.

The newcomer ordered a beer and Dockerty was reaching for the bottle when big Luke called across, 'No beer, Dockerty.'

Dockerty held up his bottle. 'But — '

'Real men drink whiskey, don't they little feller. C'mon over here and join us. Dockerty, pour the feller a double and be quick about it.'

The drummer hesitated then walked slowly across to the table. 'I'm . . . I'm sorry, gents, but I don't take whiskey.' He rubbed his mid section. 'The ulcers, you know.'

'Don't drink whiskey?' scoffed Elwood. 'Goddam but that's right unsociable. Wouldn't you say it was unsociable, bro?'

'Downright,' Luke nodded. He thrust out a big gnarled hand. 'Shake, and show us you're sociable, li'l feller.'

Reluctantly the man put out his hand. It was immediately seized in an iron grip that brought a gasp of agony from the drummer and drew a snigger of amusement from the scattered tables. The Dunstans were at it again and just about everyone, including Dockerty himself, was relieved it wasn't him Old Man's sons had for their amusement today.

'Hey, real cases them boys, ain't they, mister?' Dockerty chuckled.

Stocker's expression was blank. 'Regular vaudevillians.'

There was a thud as the drummer was forced to his knees by the pressure being exerted on his hands.

'He speaks real good, bro,' Elwood grinned. 'Hey, li'l feller, let me hear you say uncle.'

Stocker stared at his bottle. He wanted to stay neutral but this sort of thing always riled him. But more importantly, they were intruding on his hour of boozy relaxation. He glanced at the gray of dusk visible beyond the batwings and told himself it was likely time he was moving on anyway. It was many a long dry mile to Bright's City from this side of the desert.

'Git a saucer, bro! Cute li'l feller just said as how he's right partial to whiskey, after all. But only if it's from a saucer.'

Stocker diverted his attention by staring out the window and reflecting on the job ahead. He'd come a long way to reach the territory but would have been prepared to travel even further, the money they were offering. He grimaced. The money! Experience had taught him that the higher the money the greater the danger. At times when his spirit might be flagging and he got to reflecting upon the life he led, he had to remind himself anew that the gun was all he knew, the one thing in life he was good at.

The smile that creased his cheeks as he looked back over the years was humorless. He'd not moved a step without the Peacemaker within hand's reach for — how long now? He shook his head. Too long, was likely the right answer. Too much time, too many gundowns . . .

'Please! I don't know any prayers!'

'What? A real smart got-up young gent weren't taught his prayers at home? Sure you were. And me and my brother just love to hear 'em on account our mean old pappy here never taught us nothin' much 'cept how to step careful to dodge the wet copouts and how to make strangers feel to home. Come on . . . Help us Lord to be real good . . . come on, we know you know it.'

'Leave him be!'

The whiskey was reaching him and Stocker wasn't sure he'd spoken out loud until heads swung his way. The brothers bristled and Elwood let go of the ashen-faced man and wheeled to face the trouble.

'What's he say?' Old Man Dunstan said querulously.

'I said shut up and let that man be!'

Stocker was suddenly on his feet, swaying just a little but quickly stabilizing. He was riled. Even so, he knew he should stay out of this. But at the same time the gunman part of him told him a man like himself could do just about whatever he damn-well pleased — if he really wanted.

'You're still hurting him,' he said roughly as he came forward, arms swinging loosely at his sides, a big broad-shouldered figure dressed all in tan and brown. 'Let him go!'

Elwood loosened his grip and the drummer jerked clear, rolling on the floor to get away. By this time the father was on his feet hollering orders at the drinkers, and suddenly Stocker found himself confronting not just three but a dozen and more.

He almost laughed as he halted. If he hadn't shifted so much of Dockerty's lousy whiskey he might have well figured that these three were the big men in town and that most likely every working man present might well be beholden to them.

He didn't give a damn. His right palm struck gun-handle with a resounding slap.

'Back up you sons of bitches!' His voice had iron in it, whiskey and iron. He saw them falter, saw the brothers' sudden anxiety as they looked uncertainly at their father, sensing they might have blundered in out of their depth.

But the arrogant old man was eager for action. 'Sic him!' he croaked. 'Git him! What? A dozen of us agin' one saddle bum. Luke, Elwood, show him how we deal with trash in our town.'

The brothers remained exactly where they were. Stocker did not. He reached the old man in three strides. A big hand slapped hard and Pintada's leading citizen went over backwards and broke a rickety chair on his way to the floor.

It ended then and there with an ashen-faced Dockerty watching with just his eyes showing above bar level as the brothers toted the moaning old man into the back room and a dozen frozen drinkers stared.

'Gosh, thanks a million, mister. Can . . . can I buy you a drink?'

It ended there and Stocker ended up sipping beer and listening to a little traveller in utensils telling him about his childhood in Illinois over the next hour while Dockerty's regulars ordered up in subdued voices and whispered excitedly to one another as they stared at the first man ever to ride roughshod over their hated bosses.

The gunman was totally relaxed as he finally quit the place just on moonrise. He'd had his traditional pre-job drink-up but had veered off line some in buying in on something that was of no concern of his own.

Even so he was fully relaxed now and actually looking forward to getting the horse from the livery and riding off into the desert in the cool of the moonlight.

Pintada's single street appeared normal as he crossed for the livery. He glimpsed some youths strolling idly along over by the blacksmith's but took no particular notice. His fuzzy head was already beginning to clear and he was thinking of the letter addressed to him in the fine hand of Canyon County's Commissioner as he reached for the makings — then stopped on a dime.

He hadn't seen the figure beyond the livery hitch-rail when he'd started across. He was sure of it. But he was there now, a boyish silhouette, with a flashy hat thrust to the back of his head, thumbs hooked in shell belt and as relaxed looking as a puppy on a warm brick, yet somehow startling.

His hand closed over his gun butt when he realized the other youths he'd sighted had reappeared on the shadowed front porch of the general store, that yet another was now visible directly across the street.

His neck hair lifted as he backed up a pace. Alarm bells sounded. Had he been careless in tying one on in a strange town? Was one-horse Pintada really as harmless as it had looked by daylight? Suddenly he wasn't sure.

'It's OK, Stocker,' said the flashy hat. 'Just stopped by for a social word.' A silky gesture. 'Me and my buddies, that is. You got a minute to spare?'

Another long backward pace took the gunman to a point from which he could see all five without turning his head. If this proved as dangerous as it appeared, he was confident he could take out the cocky kid and maybe another one or two. But not all. They had the numbers and suddenly appeared far more dangerous than he'd figured at first glance.

'What's the name of the game?' His voice was flat and toneless.

The gunman rarely showed emotion. He carried it inside, a man who walked quietly and rode alone. An old man at thirty-four in a profession where most never lived to see the sunny side of thirty. His years in the game had given him wisdom but had not yet robbed him of either nerve or gun speed. Most times, no matter what the situation, Stocker felt instinctively he held the edge. That reassuring feeling was absent in that dragging moment, and he knew why. The whiskey.

He'd figured Pintada as a nothing town where it was safe for a man to get drunk. It was possible he was dead wrong.

'No game, big man.' The speaker raised his hand to finger back his hat as Stocker's Peacemaker slid halfway out of the oiled leather. A boyish grin. 'Hey, Chade, just take it easy. Hear?' He spread his hands. 'Hell, if we'd really wanted to dust you we could have done her easy from the windows yonder while you and the Dunstans were funning it up inside.'

'If you know who I am then you'd know I can kill you no matter what you've got backing you up, don't you, punk?'

His voice was deep. He stood like a man hewn out of oak. If the young man felt intimidated he gave no sign. He appeared totally relaxed as he came forward to lean slim hands on a horse-chewed hitch-rail.

'Name's McKidd, big man. You've heard of me mebbe?'

'No.'

Stocker was lying. The name rang a bell. But he would never concede it. With gun punks, you never gave them anything to feed their egos.

'Jesse McKidd?'

'You got something to say, say it!' Stocker made a left-handed gesture. 'The rest of you, if you're betting against me being able to handle him, then you're even younger and dumber than you look. All right, kid, what's your beef?'

'Don't go down to the capital, gunpacker!'

'What'd you say?'

'You heard.' McKidd made a lazy gesture with his right hand. 'What's going wrong in the capital is bad enough without hired iron coming into stir the pot. I'd like to think I'm saving some innocent lives, along with your own maybe, in handing out this advice.'

The gunfighter's face was stone.

'And if I tell you to go straight to hell? What then?'

Slim shoulders shrugged. 'Guess I'd be right disappointed. Why, you reckon you're likely to say something like that — old man?'

It might have been the use of the term that touched the tinder to Stocker's firebox. Then again, it could have been his own unease about this job — or most likely the half gallon of booze he'd taken aboard that caused the gunfighter to act out of character.

He grabbed for his gun.

Whether he meant to use it or simply throw a scare, he would never really know. For in that moment he was destined to relive again and again in his mind, the kid dropped his right hand and brought it up filled with gun with Stocker's weapon yet to reach shooting level.

'Don't make me drill you, old man!'

Agonizingly slow, Stocker's revolver slid back into the holster. Those final precious inches of elevation had he attempted to try for them, would have cost him his life. He knew it, as did the young man standing before him in the deepening dusk.

'You're a real pro, Stocker. Knew you would be. I didn't want to kill you, and I don't want to do it next week or next year, either. But now we understand each other, why don't you just tell yourself this is one job you don't really need to take, turn that fine palomino of yours around and head back north? Leave the desert to iron out its own troubles, huh? What do you say?'

Stocker said nothing. He appeared expressionless and calm, yet his heart was thudding against his chest wall. In eighteen years behind the gun, he'd never been outdrawn. He knew he could have died right here in this crummy crooked street — whether they attributed his death to rye whiskey or Jesse McKidd wouldn't much matter.

'Well, man, if you don't want to say nothing, at least give it some thought.' The half grin flashed. 'I don't want to kill you, and I sure as hell don't want a feller of your caliber skulking around the desert looking to kill me.' A lazy salute. 'See you when the grapes get ripe.'

He simply turned and strolled away, offering his slender back as a target. He rejoined his companions and they sauntered off into the darkness just like a bunch of young riders in town for the night, wondering how they might occupy their time.

Silence enfolded the gunfighter's powerful figure like a shroud.

* * *

He rode through the morning, the sun against his left shoulder and quickly gathering heat.

Far ahead, the haze-dusted outline of gaunt mountains told him he was on course.

But not for the county capital.

Sitting deep in his saddle, straight backed and broad shouldered, the big bronzed gunman radiated power and purpose, as always. But appearances proved deceptive this mid-morning in the desert, for Chade Stocker knew he was searching for something to restore him to full confidence.

He hadn't even been creased in the confrontation with the wild bunch in Pintada but that wasn't to say he'd escaped unscathed.

Sure, he could blame the rotgut and weariness for what had transpired. But no man who made his living with a gun could overlook the slightest first indication that he might be slipping. His life depended on knowing to within the shaved tip of a second just what he could and could not do with a .45 in a clutch situation.

Thanks to a kid who might get to shave but twice a week, his pride and vanity had taken a hit, and it hurt.

There were two sure ways a man might haul himself back from something like that. Whiskey was out. So that just left the Hard Luck Trailhouse and O'Toole's daughters.

The trailhouse, twenty miles ahead, was the farthest south he'd ever ventured into the Nogales before. It was no place for the faint-hearted or for the man with carnal intentions, Rory O'Toole being the protective and puritanical parent he was. But the daughters were nubile, Stocker knew what he wanted, so he simply kept the palomino's handsome nose pointed due south.

The heat was burning the backs of his hands. The county capital lay sixty miles away. On all sides the desert stretched away into infinity, gray, brown, tumble-weeded and monotonous. He licked dry lips and studied the dried brush that led upwards to undulating brown dunes. One jerk of the reins could take him south-west to the Mexican villages. A man could lose himself in the squalid little sheep towns, if he wanted. Get a job herding sheep, drink all he wanted and have a warm woman to come home to at night.

No guns, no uncertainty about your reflexes. Great place to hide.

He sneered. Yeah, like a grave.

*   *   *

Jesse McKidd must hang!

That sounded like an idea whose time had surely come. Leastwise that was the general impression the citizens had been given by their masters when the governor first made this ringing declaration from the balcony of the palace in Bright's City the morning after young Jesse had busted out of the jailhouse three days earlier.

Such support for the commissioner's pronouncement marked a dramatic change of sentiment in the sun-baked territory, where up until now even solid, respectable citizens with money in the bank and silver in their hair might have well reacted: Hang Jesse? Rubbish! He's just a boy sowing his wild oats . . . weren't you young and good-looking yourself once?

They weren't saying this any longer.

What they said now echoed what the governor had thundered from his balcony, namely that reckless, dashing Jesse had finally gone too far.

Busting out of the governor's jail where he'd been held on unspecified charges was bad enough. But when Jesse McKidd drove a .45 slug through Deputy Roy Murch's heart during the breakout, that nailed the lid on his casket.

The murderous incident had caused the administration's entire law enforcement capability to appear dangerously incompetent and also held the commissioner himself up to personal ridicule.

The big man would not tolerate that. Could not.

Rackage insisted that the final test of strength between law and order and the old wild ways of the past had now come when he announced a $5,000 reward on McKidd, dead or alive, then threw General Kirk and the troopers into the manhunt.

It was time for Canyon County to finally shrug off its old, almost glamorous 'Hellion Territory' mantle and don the shining new robes of peace and prosperity to carry them forward into the West's beckoning future, he declared.

That sounded disarmingly simple if you listened to Commissioner Rackage — yet many doubted that would prove to be the case.

Even so — 'Catch Jesse McKidd!'

became the cry.

In the prevailing mood of righteousness and revenge, only a few seemed totally convinced that, based on the wanted man's reputation and wide popularity in the troubled county, Jesse might very well be sporting a long gray beard before any lawman ever saw him again, much less got to catch him.

Strangely enough, one man who believed it might well prove impossible to shackle McKidd was the commissioner himself. Which was why Denver Rackage had taken highly unusual additional steps to ensure success. None but a handful of the great man's closest advisors were aware that, following the old precept of 'settin' pizen to catch a snake', administration security had sought the services of a gunfighter to boost the manhunt, a man reputed to be as fast as Jesse and one hell of a lot meaner.

That gunman's name was Stocker and security expressed a great confidence in him which the governor shared. The very name 'Stocker' seemed to carry a reassuring ring, and knowing his man was well on his way now, Commissioner Rackage finally slept well for the first time in days, the comforting image he took into his dreams that of a big bronzed gunpacker with piercing black eyes who rarely smiled, but always got his man and simply never quit.

That was an accurate enough picture of the gunfighter but scarcely a complete one. For like all men, the guntoter had his flaws. And how soundly might the commissioner have slept that night had he been aware that at that very time, his high-priced gunman was less than fifty miles distant in bed with the daughter of a half-loco religious eccentric who had shot men simply for ogling his daughters and who slept always with a double-barrel shotgun — just in case.

It was better the commissioner should sleep in ignorance on such a night, for there was little doubt he would enjoy much genuine rest now that the gunfighter was on the payroll. Stocker was that kind of man.

*   *   *

She was crying now. Stocker liked it when they cried. Added something extra, he thought.

'It's OK,' he reassured, his voice deep in the silence of her high room beneath the galvanized iron roof of the trailhouse. 'Nothin' to weep about.'

'But I feel so ashamed. I promised my father — '

'I'll handle Rory,' Stocker reassured, and meant it. The truth of it was that the girl was only half the reason he'd stopped by at the Hard Luck Trailhouse on Little Yellow Creek.

Tonight as before, he'd come here partly to draw on the owner's vast knowledge of the desert and its problems, partly to sweet-talk one of his daughters to sleep with him.

The latter urgency had to do less with simple desire than vanity.

As a gunfighter, Stocker was fast — that was a given. But his greatest strength was his self-assurance when the chips were down, a quality that had sustained him through more gundowns than he cared to remember.

But McKidd had outdrawn him.

So, before he reported for duty at Bright's City he'd felt the need to claw his way back to self-belief.

The girl was part of the cure and he reckoned it was working already. But while she drew her fingernail across his chest and nibbled his ear, the gunfighter had already returned to reality, was thinking about Crazy Rory, the danger and what his next move would be after quitting the Hard Luck, when he heard it.

The voice.

'Up here, you say? I don't see her nowhere abouts. And where did that big gunfighter git to anyway?'

He felt the girl turn cold. Her eyes were enormous in the half-light as they heard the heavy steps pause outside the door. The door rattled violently.

Dulcie had locked it. The old man began to shout and cuss and Stocker was dressing with lightning speed and wondering how far it was from the window to the ground when the miracle happened.

From the adjoining stables below came a sudden uproar of sounds, a horse kicking its stall, wild shouts, then the cry: 'Hoss thief! Hey, someone's after that palomino!'

Stocker and the petrified girl stared at one another in frozen silence as a heavy boot kicked the door again. The kicking ceased as the uproar from below increased. It seemed like an eternity before they heard the sound of heavy running steps receding down the stairs — and they began to breathe again.

Stocker was through the window and lowering himself to the landing in mere moments.

It was a full half-hour before a wild-eyed Rory O'Toole reappeared in the dimly-lit bar room below, shotgun in hand and cursing like a fool. The hostlers had saved the golden palomino but the daring would-be thief had given them the slip. Lights blazed outside and the whole place was awake and on edge, but for the bar room.

A demurely dressed Dulcie O'Toole was behind the bar pouring a double shot for a dozing Stocker who slumped deep in a heavy chair with crossed boots on a table top, frowning faintly as Crazy Rory swung his attention his way.

The shotgun stabbed at him accusingly.

'By Judas, I'd almost forgot. Just where the hell were you when I was lookin' for you, gunslinger? And you, miss, how come I couldn't find you before — '

'I've got a headache, pilgrim.' Stocker dropped boots to the floor and stared up at the frizzy-haired man with eyes like black pits. 'And you're making it worse. Last man that did that isn't annoying anyone anymore.'

Inch by inch, moment by moment, red-faced O'Toole began to deflate. The father in him was poisoned with suspicion but his practical survivor side was getting the upper hand. He hadn't seen a more dangerous man than the one occupying his best chair, had never before had the experience of Chade Stocker giving him that stare.

It still seemed a long slow time before his Adam's apple bobbed and he found his voice.

'Guess I was a little over-heated, er . . . Mr Stocker. No offence.' Then sharply. 'Girl, bring the man a drink at the double. Hop to it!'

'That's more like it,' Stocker growled, still hardfaced. 'Now set down and tell me what I need to know about the county before I go poking my nose in down at the capital, Rory.'

'Sure, boy, what is it you'd like to be knowin'?'

Everything.

* ★ ★

He was ten miles out along the faint
trace of the trail by first light. Back
there, a girl was dabbing tears from her
eyes, her father was sleeping off a
hangover, and out here Chade Stocker
had a lot on his mind.

From what he'd learned back at
Pintada and the trailhouse, it appeared
the situation in the desert might be
much worse even than he'd expected
— so he mused as the palomino carried
him into the new morning. Corruption,
uncertainty, power-faction rivalries and
a growing tally of the dead, these were
common enough afflictions in many a
raw and half-settled sector of the West,
yet he was faintly surprised that a man
of Rackage's reputation would allow it
to happen here.

He shrugged and rode on, feeling the
sun warmer on his shoulders, relaxed as
tobacco smoke drifted over his shoulder
and he idly stroked his clean-shaven
cheek. Yet he was alert as a man of his

calling must always be, and so sighted the overturned stone to one side of the trail where another man might have seen nothing.

He kept on riding but now his right hand rested on gun butt in a seemingly casual way while in the shadow of his hatbrim dark eyes raked the way ahead.

The reason he'd noticed the pebble was that it was darker than those surrounding it. It was darker because it had been recently overturned to expose its dark underside.

Directly ahead stood a cluster of trailside boulders beneath a gaunt and ugly cottonwood. The hot wind blew, shadows stirred, but what caught his eye and held it was not a tree shadow, but the faintest glint of hot light on something metallic.

He reined in and the Peacemaker was in his big brown hand.

'Show yourself before I blow you to hell!'

No response. He cocked the piece and raised it to eye level. He could no longer see any movement, but was able to figure where the man had to be. If he put enough lead into that niche it would have to bring the dry-gulcher to his feet — and then he would kill him. No second thoughts. Not out here on a lonesome stretch of trail, with thoughts of the McKidd bunch still fresh in his mind, there wasn't.

His finger was compressing the trigger when the runty figure exploded from the rocks, hands grabbing sky, voice raised in panic.

'For the love of the Holy Mother, don't be shootin' a man for nothin' at all.'

He was Irish, claimed his name was Moran, insisted it had been fear not evil intent that had driven him to cut for cover upon sighting him after having been left stranded when his horse ran off in the night.

Stocker eyed him suspiciously as he returned to his niche and reappeared leading an ugly, slab-sided mule. The man looked sharp, quick and crooked, he thought. Then suspicion hit and he angled the six-shooter at him again.

'That was you, wasn't it?' he growled.

'Me what? Can I be for puttin' me hands down before I — '

'Why else would I find you here afoot in walking distance of the trailhouse if you're not the bastard who tried to steal my horse?'

'Who be you?'

'You be dead if you don't own up — '

'All right, all right, you got me dead to rights. But it is such a wonderful horse and me bein' down on me luck and all — '

'Start walking. You can tell your story when we get to the junction.'

'But it's fifty miles and — '

'Move!'

But the runt stood his ground, something cunning crossing his punched-in mug now. 'I'll do as you say, Mister Stocker — '

'You know my name? How?'

'I was on the roof.'

Stocker's frown cut deep. 'What?'

Now the other was smiling: it wasn't a good smile. 'The evil O'Toole had a feller guardin' the stable, so I climbed up on the roof next door to find me way in, you see. I'm the best and quietest climber you ever did see, Mr Stocker, sir. As for me hearin' and eyesight, even at night . . . well, let me tell you that, what with you bein' so busy and all, and the moonlight kind of spillin' into that room . . . ' He grinned and spread his hands. 'Well, all I can say is I envy you, lad, although in a way I'd be terrible scared if I was in your boots for fear that some gabby Irishman might spill what he saw to the sheriff, and if it got back to Crazy Rory . . . '

His words faded. He stood in the road like a smirking leprechaun and Stocker's features were unreadable as his thoughts raced ahead. He knew the bastard was telling the truth, just as he was certain he would carry out his threat, given the motive and opportunity. He could handle Crazy Rory blindfolded and unarmed, he knew. But the trailhouse boss hadn't come by his nickname without reason. The man was just mad enough to hand his daughter a flogging then broadcast word of Stocker's 'rape', which was probably how he'd choose to interpret it, all over the county. Normally that wouldn't bother him, but an uproar like that could well jeopardize his position as the governor's protector and see him recalled.

He had too much pride for that.

He clicked his gun hammer but the smirking horse-thief was calmly twisting a cigarette. He winked, and the gunman's face was stone as he shoved the Peacemaker away.

'Start walking.'

The horse-thief didn't so much walk, as skip.

2

Wild Boys Riding

The riders came in out of the raddled hills on a day when the sun flooded earth in infinite fire. Across the shimmering miles there was no other sign of life, no reptiles, birds, wild mustangs or prairie dogs waiting to scold the intruders into their domain. The bunch comprised of five lithe-bodied horsemen who, incongruously, were singing in close harmony as their ponies clop-hoofed by a bleak saguaro and on towards the great stack of strange black stones which the desert Indians called God's Eggs.

It was an old song and they knew all the words as they sang:

'I've labored long and hard for bread

For honor and for riches
But on my corn's you've trod too
long
You fine-haired sons of bitches.'

The voices faded away and the youngest of the group, a stripling of no more than eighteen, squinted against the glare and said, 'You want someone to climb atop the Eggs to take a look-around, Jesse?'

'Don't sweat it, man. Ain't nobody who'd venture this far out on a day like this if I was worth fifty thousand, never mind just a crummy five.'

The young rider laughed. They weren't outlaws, just friends of Jesse McKidd's. Yet they were unique in the same way that caused McKidd to stand out, in so far as they were not just young but zestfully, exuberantly so in a way few others were or could be even if they'd wanted.

Work was less than a passion for them, while their respect for authority or their betters was at best a day-to-day proposition. They were wild and foot-loose and inclined toward trouble, but until that summer season in the south, none had ever been seriously wanted by the law, certainly none, not even fast Jesse, had ever had a noose waiting for him should he ever show up in the capital again.

His friends were deeply impressed both by what McKidd was alleged to have done and by the way he was handling the consequences.

With half Canyon County scouring the brush for him and the other half defending him fiercely, McKidd might be expected to show at least a flicker of anxiety or concern, maybe even suggest heading for the mountains or maybe the Mex border until things cooled down. His henchmen would not have regarded such a reaction as any kind of weakness, for none was sleeping well at night simply knowing they were riding with the most wanted man in the territory. Yet Jesse continued to eat like a horse, sleep like a baby and was keeping his pony's nose pointed south by south west as they used up the long horse miles with the easy air of someone without one blessed problem in the blue-eyed world.

South by south-west lay a town. The bunch loved towns, but McKidd's companions today feared that any town any place could be nothing but dangerous right now.

Of course, none of them had thought that his fronting that big gunfighter up at Pintada was such a swell idea at the time, yet somehow they seemed to have survived the experience.

Stocker had scared the hell out of Enoch, Dakota, Frenchy and Wiley, yet it was almost as if Jesse had forgotten all about the man with the tied-down Peacemaker.

McKidd kept right on humming a tune, swatting at the flies and occasionally flexing his supple back to ease the saddle strain, until the snub-nosed youth on the appaloosa had to break the silence.

'You really figure he means it, Jesse?' he asked as though he really needed to know.

'Huh?'

McKidd sounded dreamy. There were times when he was so sharply focused and intelligent that he seemed able to guess what a man was going to say even before he spoke, but equally as often the wild rider dreamed, smiling off into some secret realm of his own where there was no heat and sand or bloody gun battles, and certainly no powerful men sitting about in old palaces fulminating against him and baying for his blood.

This was such a moment, yet McKidd still seemed to be dreaming as he gazed off into the heat-stricken distances towards Rifleburg and privately jousted with whatever dragons, shining knights or dark-visaged villains that might people his fantasy world, which at times could seem more hard-edged and real to him than the one he lived in — this world of the south-west which this youth seemed bent on molding into his own chosen shape.

At times like this he seemed just like the personable young hero so many folks seemed to want him to be. If nothing else, McKidd at least looked the part the territory had mapped out for him.

But something had recently gone wildly awry with this image. A jail door hung open, a man lay dead and they were baying for his blood. And now he was being asked if everything they'd heard about his past hair-raising week was real.

Shrugging his way out of his reverie of sand, sun and sky, he looked at his questioner in calm sobriety. Then he nodded.

'Sure, he means it right enough, pard. Commissioners don't joke, you know.'

'But nobody believes you'd cut anybody down that way, man,' weighed in another. He paused then added,

'Any more than most would believe . . . you know . . . about you and the commissioner's lady.'

'It's true, I'm sorry to say, man,' said McKidd. 'At least some of it is.'

'You did kill that guard?' he was asked.

'No, not that. Someone shot him, but it wasn't me. But the other is a fact, I guess.'

Again they were silenced. McKidd might be wild but was no philanderer. The admission that he may have broken his own code with the wife of the all-powerful county commissioner left some a little breathless.

Yet, this admission only seemed to serve to garnish his legend in the eyes of the others. Where they were men who seemed incapable of doing just about anything right, McKidd, by contrast was held by surprisingly many to be rarely ever wrong. Not even when they said he'd killed a man and had an affair with the commissioner's lady.

'Guess Rackage would figure out by about now that they ain't likely to catch you, eh, Jesse?'

'Could do, Frenchy,' he replied, shifting his weight in the saddle. 'Only thing, the commissioner figures he has to win every hand. He's that sort of man. Caroline, that's his wife, she told me so. So I guess he'll just keep after me until either he catches me or I weary of it all and head for Mexico.'

'Ain't you leavin' out one thing, man?'

'What's that, Enoch?'

'You could save yourself a whole mess of trouble by going after Rackage,' came the harsh reply.

'Don't be crazy man,' McKidd reproved mildly. 'You don't kill county commissioners.'

'He's sure tryin' to kill you.'

McKidd could not argue with that. So he gave his horse a kick, clicked the reins.

'We're coming down with desert rot. Let's make some time.'

'Still for Rifleburg?' Wiley asked apprehensively.

'Why not?' came McKidd's reply, and led the way south at the lope.

There were no lawmen or bounty hunters present in one-horse Rifleburg when they arrived, just a lot of towners wearing their Sunday best and a huge cake occupying pride of place on the bar of the Last Post Saloon that was ornamented with nineteen candles and the words HAPPY BIRTHDAY DAKOTA! spelled out in sickly pink icing.

Turned out Jesse had arranged it all by telegraph ahead of time and not even the biggest man hunt in a decade was going to keep him from celebrating his pal's big day.

Jesse predicted the party would roll all night long, and it did. This was due both to the fact that he said so, and also because he simply made it work. That was McKidd's way. Small wonder half the territory was rooting for him while the other half mostly wanted to.

This smiling, gun-quick boy was loved in a way no commissioner ever could hope to be. Yet in the euphoria of the big party night it was easy to overlook the fact that Denver Rackage commanded power such as boys like them could only dream of. An even more ominous fact of life was that the most dominant personality in the entire county was a proud man wronged.

*   *   *

'Who's complaining about his dead jackass?'

The gaunt man with the drooping mustache and military bearing emerged from the doorway leading from the inner sanctum, the commissioner's chambers. He stood facing a 100 foot long paneled corridor, crowded by men and women, mostly men. It was like this every day, and every day Bob Clutterloe had to deal with them. 'The dead jackass!' he shouted, shaking a fistful of documents. 'Where is he?'

A ragged figure stepped forward, clutching a piece of paper. He was a man of the land, small, wiry and burnt by the sun.

'All right,' barked the commissioner's man, 'What happened to your lousy mule?'

'It died because my neighbor let the run-off from his mine spill into my creek, Mr Clutterloe, sir. I've . . . I've come to the governor for compensation.'

Clutterloe's nostrils flared. It was like a disease, he fumed. A new commissioner comes in and every ragged-assed no-account has a gripe, every man-Jack of them with his hand out looking to the great man to solve their every problem and hand them money like he was Santa Claus.

He looked around. They circled him like buzzards, each waiting to watch how he dealt with the dead jackass to get a line on how his individual claim, grab, con or twister might go.

He stared the farmer in the eye and

said. 'Nice try. Now get lost.'

The mob buzzed. Clutterloe was in a mood today. The runty farmer hung his head, started to back away but another man, larger and more assured-looking stepped forward.

'That ain't fair, Mr Clutterloe. Johnson's got a valid claim here. Without his jackass he ain't gonna be able to work his land and he cain't afford to buy another. The commissioner's gotta stand by him.'

'Yeah,' chorused some onlookers, and one spoke up: 'Didn't Rackage say he'd look after the little man?'

But Clutterloe kept his eye on the tall fellow. He was a troublemaker who made his way here most every day, always outspoken, always riding some malcontent's hobby horse for him. The tall man met his eye defiantly and Bob Clutterloe had suddenly had enough. Raising his right hand he adjusted the stickpin holding his plain dark tie.

It was a signal.

Immediately from an alcove where

they had been seated sipping coffee stepped four burly men in uniform led by Sergeant Bourke.

The tall man tried to duck away but the sergeant was too quick. He seized him by the arm and jerked him roughly. The tall man swore and tried to break free.

'Assault upon an officer,' Bourke shouted, and the corporal drove his truncheon into the man's kidneys, causing him to sag at the knees. The others grabbed him and he was whisked away, the whole incident occupying no longer than a handful of seconds.

Now the long corridor was quiet. Clutterloe occupied the center of it. He raised his documents and said challengingly, 'Next! Who the hell is next?'

Silence.

Then a flunkey appeared with an odd look on his homely face and said, 'Stocker, sir.'

Clutterloe glared. 'What did you say?'

'The name's Stocker, soldier boy.'

The troopers swung in the direction

of the voice to see that a big man had moved into the room. His shoulders were broad and his hips were narrow. Both hair and eyes were black as midnight and he wore a single long-barreled revolver on the right hip. A smoking cigar jutted from his teeth and his attitude reflected a kind of arrogance which simply wasn't in keeping with the approved manner of any supplicant who arrived here to seek audience with the commissioner of the county.

The troopers looked at Clutterloe, who uncharacteristically hesitated. He was a man of authority and used it freely. There wasn't one thing he liked about this stranger at first glance and in the mood he was in today he was ready to flick his tie-pin and see the big bastard thrown out, his runty sidekick with him.

And yet he hesitated. Surely there was something about this man that proclaimed him very different from any supplicant. Something intimidating.

The dark eyes were fixed on Clutterloe in a way that warned him to caution, told him not to overplay his hand until he knew just exactly who he was or what game he was playing.

'Chade Stocker to see Rackage,' the stranger stated. 'Better see to it, boy.'

Stocker! Clutterloe thought, raking him up and down. He should have guessed.

'I'll go see if the commissioner can see you,' he said sourly.

'Sure he'll see me. Tell him I don't like to be kept waiting.'

All eyes were on the newcomer as the door closed on Clutterloe's back. They were wary, even the surly troopers who clustered in a corner, whispering. Stocker was accustomed to having this effect. He liked it. Stocker liked it. Making friends or good impressions never got a man anywhere when on an assignment, he believed. Scared people or men who hated your guts were far more likely to make mistakes or maybe spill something they shouldn't. Already, he figured he would need all the help he could get here to get a line on McKidd.

Seemed this runaway killer was something of a hero around Bright's City.

Stocker hated heroes. Particularly if they happened to be younger than he and better looking. Or, as was quite possible in the case of young Jesse McKidd, the hero was faster with a Colt .45.

* * *

McKidd whistled softly in the baking heat of a desert noon. The wide brown river was turning before him like a sleepy snake, running down the hills from the north-west and he followed its course to the bridge at the south end of Oak Flats.

He stopped at the bridge and broke open his .45 to check the loads. He squinted at the brassy ball of the sun that looked at the town.

Everything looked normal enough,

but these days a man could never be sure. Crossing the bridge, he circled around the frame and adobe mining town, looking for a sign. Not a humdrum, everyday sign, but tracks or clues that might indicate that 'they' had been around.

The man hunters.

The men who killed for money, even those ready to do it out of spite.

The commissioner's men.

There was nothing but everyday tracks of horses and wagons to be found, and suddenly McKidd was impatient, turning the nose of his appaloosa directly toward the town.

Despite his notoriety he was an easygoing fellow with a ready smile for most everybody, but that grin was missing today. Days on the dodge had shown just how serious Rackage was this time. He'd seen more posse men than there were sheep up on the Greasy Grass Hills. This time they really wanted him. That was OK. But there was no way one posseman or five hundred was going to hinder his freedom. This was his land, there was a friend in Oak Flats he wanted to visit, and he was going to do it.

The streets were hot and dusty with just a sprinkling of people abroad in the heat.

Mostly they smiled and waved at the slender rider, yet before making it to the central block, McKidd found himself turning constantly, raking streets and alley mouths with narrowed eyes, massaging the back of his neck.

Was there something not quite right in the atmosphere, or was wild Jesse McKidd finally beginning to exhibit signs of on-the-dodge nerves? This thought peeved him and he swung in at the general store, looped his reins over the hitch-rack and started up the steps.

He halted.

It really was uncommonly still; he wasn't just imagining it. Dust devils danced lazily and it seemed an old shire-horse eyed him too steadily.

Heat waves rose in ripples off the

street and McKidd felt a trickle of perspiration course down his spine. Now he was sorry he'd gotten down. He should have gone with his instincts and kept riding. What had been an uneasy hunch was now a clamor of nerve ends. He was certain something wasn't right and decided he must not step inside but should rather turn and get back to his horse. He was man enough to admit that such a public backdown would go hard against the grain, yet he was prepared to do it.

Yet he delayed defiantly, daring trouble to show itself, suddenly angry at the situation Rackage and his minions had forced him into.

Then it happened.

Across the street, a door burst open and a little girl some six or seven years of age, came rushing out, skirt and pigtails flying, screaming.

'Jesse! They're here! They're here!'

He didn't even know her but vaguely recognized the white-faced woman who came running from the store to reclaim her. He had about the shaved tip of a second to haul his shooter before gunflame erupted from a window across the street. Lethal lead whipped above his head and he instantly dived low.

His gun roared twice, the shots snarling deep-throated and flattening across the empty street. He held his fire as window glass tinkled to floorboards. A long moment passed. Then the heavy body came sliding through the broken window like a bag of suet pouring onto the walk like something without bones, the shattered skull glistening crimson.

The stutter of running feet. McKidd was up and taking giant strides across the street to reach the mouth of the alley mere moments before the second gunman would have cleared it at the far end. He shot him through the back of the head. The man threw up his gun and pivoted slowly before bending at the hips and hitting the weeds with his face.

The Crogan brothers.

He recognized them both. Scum, but scum he'd shared some times with. Now corrupted by the commissioner's money and ready to swallow his lies. He was no killer, but Rackage was turning him into one. He didn't move as he heard doors slowly open . . . then footsteps all around him. Once he'd had nothing to fear from the regular citizens of places like White Oaks. They were plain folks, like himself. Only difference now, Rackage was going all out to put him in his grave, and the whole county knew it.

He wondered momentarily, almost desperately, if it might not save him a lot of grief to simply throw a leg over his pony, ride down to the capital and blow Rackage to hell.

He dismissed the thought but it would come again.

3

Pray for a Killer

Stocker was impressed.

Not thirty feet from where they sank into the luxury of deep leather chairs set up on opposite sides of a mahogany desk a good fifteen feet long, reality was making its presence felt at the palace of the county commissioner's headquarters on the square.

Outside along the corridor they wandered in and out, the poor and the complaining, the rogues and rebels, the wary and the seeking, the strayed, the defeated, the careless and the already doomed. All came hopeful to the palace even though fully aware that few, if any, would leave with one thing more than they came with.

But hope sprang eternal, and this man seated opposite the gunman had given them hope. Stocker had already realized that Rackage was a huge disappointment to the people who'd voted him in, which was likely the cause of all the instability and uncertainty he'd seen here. But the poor weren't his concern. Denver Rackage and his enemies were.

Rackage had proven different from what he'd imagined, being taller and more rugged than he'd expected of a man of his high office.

He met the gaze directly and seemed to radiate a restless energy even when seated, as he finished summarizing the McKidd situation for his benefit. Stocker sat motionless studying the man keenly through a haze of tobacco smoke.

The man with the reputation for nurturing a big vision for Canyon County, Rackage was also reputed as a leader who knew how to communicate, inspire, lead by example. He'd plainly familiarized himself with Stocker's record which encompassed some quite remarkable achievements offset by instances of the careless and excessive. Rackage was neither critical nor flattering as he made it plain that he considered Stocker the perfect man for the job and had hand-picked him from the talent available from a wide variety of sources, while expressing no interest in the less savory aspect of the gunfighter's career or character. The commissioner had sent for him immediately following McKidd's escape from lawful custody.

This unusual decision had been prompted by the fear that the man might prove both too elusive and too well supported by the populace to be easily apprehended by the usual means. Such had proven to be the case and the big man seemed highly pleased with his own initiative in securing Stocker's services.

His job description sounded simple enough. Catch McKidd, the chore that had proven too much for both law and army.

What did he say?

'I'm here, ain't I?'

Rackage eyed him coldly. 'That's not an answer.'

'It is to me.' He wasn't sure why he was speaking this way. Maybe he found Rackage too self-assured and superior for his taste.

'It's possible you don't like me, Stocker.'

'Possible.'

'Well, that doesn't matter a damn to me. I make friends and enemies. Right now, my enemies are making life difficult. I hired you because your record indicates you're the man to take this gun kid out of the equation. You should feel proud I picked you out. You are the chosen gun.'

His eyebrows lifted. The chosen gun. Had almost an ominous ring to it, he thought.

He relaxed. 'OK, I'm your man. Tell me more about this kidling.'

He had no qualms about going after someone so many viewed as a noble native son while the other half appeared fearful of him. Neither did he worry that the killer might well come hunting him once he'd officially signed on to hunt him down. Naturally he'd made no reference to the fact that he'd already encountered his quarry under the strangest of strange circumstances.

There was nothing to be gained by brooding about whether it had been the whiskey that had beaten him that night . . . or Jesse McKidd. In his profession, self-confidence could prove far more important than gun speed, and his had returned, in full measure.

'So, having cleared that up, I suppose I can accept the fact that you consider yourself up to what is admittedly a highly dangerous task?'

He met the man's eyes levelly. 'I can take this man.'

This seemed to please Rackage. 'Well, I'm comforted by the fact that your record indicates you're exceptionally gifted at the killing business.'

'Tolerably, I guess.'

'Uh huh. So tell me this. How would you feel if I told you I wanted McKidd taken alive?'

Stocker's surprise showed plain. 'Why?'

Rackage rose and beckoned him to join him at the huge windows overlooking the square. Trade barrows, stalls, horses and scores of people crowded the wide area. The palace gates were heavily guarded by riflemen in shabby gray uniforms. Stocker didn't need to be told he was viewing a tense and uneasy city.

'McKidd is viewed by many as some kind of youthful symbol of the county's future. But unfortunately my political enemies have quite cynically boosted this boy up to represent the opposition to my administration and everything I'm pledged to achieve. Their stratagem has worked and the outlaw has assumed a ridiculously high status in the eyes of many. That is why I want him brought back, tried, found guilty and dealt with by law and in public before being executed like the common criminal he is. Only if it's handled that way will the people be satisfied. This procedure will effectively destroy the baseless and dangerous myths surrounding the man along with the man himself. Do I make myself plain?'

It could scarce be plainer.

Chade nodded and reached for his hat. He paused.

'When McKidd busted out of jail. What was he in for?'

Rackage's brows lifted in surprise. 'Why do you ask?'

'I like to know the full background when I go to work on a job.'

'Well, if you must know . . . it was rather a combination of offences rather than one specific crime. Rebellious behaviour, several suspected cattle thefts, brawling . . . the usual things you'd expect from somebody like him.'

'In other words, he was arrested for nothing much?'

The big man's displeasure showed

plain. 'Is there a point to this, Mr Stocker?'

'I've heard McKidd didn't expect to leave your jail alive. Some say he got arrested for just horsing around . . . but the law aimed to hang him . . . '

'Perhaps I've been misinformed about you, Stocker,' Rackage replied stiffly. 'I was not warned that you might prove to be a bleeding heart, even worse, a McKidd sympathizer.'

Stocker didn't reply immediately. He was studying the tall man's face. For just a moment, something ruthless and dangerous flickered in steel-gray eyes and he realized the county commissioner could be a dangerous adversary.

He filed the thought for future reference. His features remained expressionless. 'Just curious. A good player always likes to know if there's a joker in the deck.'

'There's nothing underhand or unstated about your assignment. We're simply dealing with an outlaw whom I believe means me great harm. It starts and ends there.'

'Fine, I'll keep you posted on how I'm progressing.'

'Fine.'

★ ★ ★

Their meeting at an end, the commissioner ushered his visitor from his chambers into the huge ante-room. Stocker found himself confronted by a vast expanse of parquet floors, lofted ceilings, a thirty-foot high window overlooking an interior parade ground, barracks, outbuildings and a sand-covered horse-yard where he caught a glimpse of a young woman riding a palfrey.

Surly attendants in military gray guarded each set of doors to the echoing chamber. All snapped to attention and saluted briskly upon Rackage's appearance. A husky young sergeant appeared from a side door. He clicked booted heels and said, 'All in order, sir?'

'Yes, Donovan. Mr Stocker is now

officially on the government payroll and is to be accorded any assistance he might require.'

Donovan shot Stocker a guarded look. 'If you say so, Commissioner. Er, there's a wire . . . '

'Well, let me see it, man.' Rackage turned sharply. 'Who the devil is that?'

Donovan made to reply but paused as someone cursed fluently. Heads turned and Stocker sighted Moran plainly involved in an argument with an attendant.

'Just my dogsbody,' he supplied. 'Name's Moran. He's troublesome but harmless.'

His decision to allow the bum to journey to the capital with him had been sound, he believed. For despite the fact that Irish Dave Moran was a horse thief and drunk and almost certainly had many other personality defects, he had revealed certain usable qualities which Stocker could employ. The Irishman was shrewd, quick and enterprising and was proving a fount of information regarding the county and its more colorful characters and was a general asset, at least while sober.

Rackage said nothing as he took the yellow telegraph slip from the husky sergeant, who shot Stocker a narrow look.

'Hmm,' the commissioner murmured after a moment. 'Most strongly object . . . brawling in a public place . . . intimidating behaviour . . . ' He paused in his reading, raised brows at Stocker. 'This is from the mayor of Pintada, Mr Stocker. It's about you.'

'Just a friendly dust-up.'

'Sounds much more than that to me,' put in Donovan. 'Commissioner, surely this is hardly a recommendation, is it? I mean — '

'Take your file and . . . file it, Sergeant,' Rackage snapped. 'I'm hiring a man I believe can handle a job which neither you nor your entire regiment has proven capable of doing. If I'd wanted some milksop yes-man I'd have hired one. Remember that and just follow orders. Hear?'

The husky Donovan went off, face burning hotter when he turned to see Stocker smirking after him contemptuously. The gunfighter made enemies easily. He considered this an asset in his trade, for it kept him on his toes.

It was not customary for the commissioner to show guests out personally, but as though to emphasize Stocker's status now, Rackage set about guiding him from the ante-room into a lobby off which ran the enormous, crowded corridor.

Instantly the hissing began.

During his audience with Rackage, Stocker's presence had been revealed to the petitioners. Most hated him instantly, for the news that a gunman had been hired to get McKidd had been leaked somehow. The mob felt emboldened by its numbers and there were vulgar gestures and clicking teeth to show him what they thought of any low killer who could be hired to go after a true blue hero like Jesse McKidd.

Stocker was impassive.

He could never be intimidated by any mob. He waved and flashed a big smile as though deliberately misinterpreting their reaction.

'You should be ashamed of yourself, Sir!' a red-faced derelict shouted at Rackage, shaking a fist. 'Even if Jesse done wrong, he don't deserve to have this kind of butcher souled onto him.'

'See what I mean?' Rackage said as they crossed the polished floors for the final set of double doors. 'I'm pitted not just against a man but an empty myth.' He halted at the doors, rested a hand on Stocker's forearm, spoke earnestly. 'I'm placing my confidence in you at a critical time in the county's history, you won't let me down, will you?'

'I'll get him, I said.'

'Alive?'

'Sure, if it's possible.'

'Perhaps I was vaguely amused by that report from Pintada, Mr Stocker. But I hope there'll be no more of that

sort of behaviour during this assignment?'

'Bet on it.'

Catching up and swaggering after
them, Moran muffled a snort at this.
Stocker shot him a warning look. For
he was serious. From the outset, he'd
intended playing this one straight down
the line. He must. He was running low
on funds and his last job had proven
messy and unresolved, damaging to the
reputation. So this one would be
different, for there was always a
concern that his hell-raising could lead
to his not being taken as seriously as he
needed to be in his trade.

He quit the palace in an upbeat
mood only to come face to face with a
city which wasn't always welcoming to
strangers with guns.

★ ★ ★

The big heavy chair broke into a dozen
flying fragments as it came crashing
down across Stocker's shoulders. More

disgusted than hurt, he whirled and let loose a right which travelled a bare six inches before exploding into the bloated, punched-in mug of the black-smith striker. The chair-wielder's mouth spewed claret and he fell into the mêlée of drinkers struggling to get at free-swinging Stocker, and those fighting even more strenuously to escape from him.

His well-aimed kick caught an attacker square in the crotch. The man crumpled screaming to the bar room floor and Stocker deliberately stamped on his head. Why not? He'd been simply having a quiet beer in a shadowed corner of this anonymous bar, smoking a cigarette and not making any trouble — when the United Brotherhood of the Friends and Admirers of Jesse McKidd — their unofficial title — came in on him like a tidal wave.

He would never stand still for that. He didn't.

A fist glanced harmlessly off the side

of his temple. Stocker smoothly scooped up a fifth of Old Uncle Chris bourbon, broke it over the man's hard head then playfully jabbed him in the face with it.

The man screamed like a stuck hog and Cindy blew the whistle that she kept on a golden chain slung around her neck and tucked between breasts the size and sensual firmness of ripened cantaloupes.

Up until then Stocker hadn't realized that the statuesque beauty ran this bar, or that her authority here seemed absolute. It seemed the bar mistress had been content to let the boys have their fun with the newcomer, but felt obliged to draw the line now when he looked like handing out one hell of a lot more than he got.

'Put a lid on this and clean up this mess, pronto!' she bawled in a voice that caused the rafter spiders to go scuttling for their holes.

Stocker didn't blame the critters. His unmarked face wore a wry look as he mopped off sweat with a spotted bandanna and took several deep breaths while Cindy's people enforced the peace then cleared away the fallen. If she thought this was a serious ruckus, she had a lot to learn.

Even so he'd been riled to find himself in trouble again a mere few hours since assuring both Rackage and himself to low key his introduction into the life of the troubled capital.

But maybe, he mused, it had been a tad confrontational on his part to visit a known McKidd haunt so early on, knowing the city's mood?

'Are you leavin' now?' Cindy asked tersely when peace reigned once again.

'No. Are you?'

She glared, then relaxed. They began to talk. Some time later he casually told her she was a knockout, and they got along a little better from that point on. Yet he knew that was the best he might expect here — just getting along.

Finally he bought a round for the bar, chucked Cindy under the chin, pinched her bottom and meandered off to inspect this great cave-like barn of a place. He was familiarizing himself with Bright's City, absorbing the conflicting pro and anti-McKidd atmosphere, testing the water and searching for leads; almost any old lead on his quarry would be welcome right now.

It was amazing how much an observant man could pick up in a short space of time simply by watching and listening. He encouraged a bunch of young cowboys to assure him that Jesse McKidd would certainly never cut and run just because some 'hotshot man-hunter' had been imported to run him down. Others, by contrast, insisted it was high time the commissioner carried the fight to the hellions, and he nodded in apparent agreement with them also.

While appraising Canyon County he was also making his plans.

He'd already decided to concentrate his manhunt to within a fifty-mile radius of the capital, first up. He based this on information that painted the fugitive as gutsy and defiant, the kind who'd be highly unlikely to go hole up in a cave in the San Cristos upon hearing a hired gun was after him, but rather might stick around and defy him to do his worst. Maybe the characteristics he'd sensed in the man who'd braced him outside Dockerty's Saloon that night might eventually trip the cocky kid up and enable him to slip the noose around his skinny neck, providing he played his cards right.

He was not selling his man short, that would be stupid. McKidd had a rep and it was solid. He was ten years Stocker's junior and — as various drunks assured him and as he had discovered personally — 'faster than a ghost skatin' on winter ice'.

When he made his easy way back to Cindy's corner of the bar she treated him to a drink and he enquired casually what she might know about places like Starr Hollows, Claybank and the exotic sounding Shaman's Canyon.

Cindy leaned her elbows on the bar to make the most of her cleavage.

'Wastin' your time, handsome. You won't find him there or any of the other places the losers might have told you about.'

'You another Jesse lover, I take it?'

'Just a life-lover, big feller. And I've seen enough of both Jesse and the commissioner to know that gettin' caught up between them two could buy anyone a one-way ticket to Boot Hill. And that was even before you showed up through the tall grass. Guess you'd better believe I'm too young and raunchy and fond of life to be fool enough to count Rackage, Jesse or your good-lookin' self as anything but passers-by . . . ships in the night. That answer your question?'

He just grinned and sipped his drink as chastened and mostly silent drinkers stared at him morosely from the surrounding tables. They'd tested his mettle and their numerous cuts, bruises and one slinged arm testified to the cost. Now they seemed resigned to sit back simply and watch, nursing their resentment.

Resentment ran deep in Bright's City; he'd already been here long enough to know that.

On one hand the rancher, miner and man in the street seemed grudgingly admiring of the way the Rackage administration had improved commerce and trade, cleaned up much of the general outlawry and crime and attracted outside finance, vital to the hitherto neglected region's progress.

But all this at a cost, so it seemed.

Having met the commissioner and some of his top people, Stocker had come away with the clear impression of a strong man probably bordering on the ruthless. It was easy enough to picture Rackage pressing on headlong with his ambitious agenda of self-promotion with scant regard for those who might be mangled in the process.

He was told in a bar that once, in his cups, Rackage had bragged what his career path would prove to be — county commissioner, territorial governor, US senator — in that order. At the same time he'd described Canyon County as a cesspit he expected to leave behind him just as soon as he quelled the 'insurrection' typified in his mind by McKidd.

The resentment against the administration was now almost palpable, which he supposed went at least part of the way towards explaining the popularity of McKidd.

He scowled. What wagon masters, storekeepers, hard-scrabble cattlemen and the city man in the street imagined to be just some wild kid and a bunch of boys having a high old time, appeared to be a long way different from the reality, he mused.

Apart from the defiance of McKidd, rustling was still endemic here, furious gun battles could erupt any place, any time. For every citizen who proclaimed Commissioner Rackage the best thing that ever happened in Nogales Desert there was another clamoring for a native, home-grown natural leader to be handed the reins — even if most of these might concede that 'contender' McKidd was likely about twenty-two years too young for the post — apart from being wanted on a murder charge.

Refining his thoughts, Stocker supposed that, had he been the commissioner in the situation he'd found himself, he would have sent for someone exactly like Chade Stocker.

He'd seen it proven many times in many places. When a ranch, a town, a region or even a government defied the best efforts of well-meaning men to change, the solution was to wheel in a Masterton, a Hickok — or a Stocker. It might be messy for a spell, and certainly dangerous. But there was a good chance that when it was over a young woman could stroll down Main Street at midnight in her skivvies and nobody would dare lay a hand on her fine pink hide.

Peace in our time

He raised his glass to them all and was deciding between ordering another or grabbing an early night when the creaking of batwings heralded a late arrival.

'And the top of the evenin' to every single tosspot of you all,' Irish Dave greeted cheerily. He paused in mock astonishment to watch a swamper toting out a pile of lumber which until recently had been a sturdy chair, cut a wry look at the big figure leaning on the bar. 'To be sure, let me be for guessing. All that your handiwork, Mr Stocker sir?'

A combination of a satisfying ruckus, some good sipping whiskey, and Cindy's rosy bosom to appreciate all had Stocker feeling relaxed. He didn't want anybody spoiling his mood.

'You can drop the Emerald Isle act,' he said. 'What do you want?'

'Well, perhaps you've forgot you want me off to sniff around and see what I could learn?'

'Okay, what?'

The ragged Irishman leaned on the bar. He was actually sober.

'Well, the news has come through that the gentleman you're interested in has shot and killed a pair of bounty-hunters.'

A sudden silence fell. A pale-faced Cindy leaned across her bartop. 'You sure about this?'

'The city marshal told me personally, me darlin'.' Moran swung to study Stocker's face. 'That bad enough for you?'

'What else?'

Moran leaned close to the gunfighter and whispered: 'That story was all malarkey. What I really come to tell you is that in the alley out the back with the darkness and the tomcats, there's a pretty woman waitin' to see you.'

Stocker drained his glass. He had no way of knowing if the report on McKidd was true or not. He reckoned the notion of any woman being eager to meet him in some dark alleyway was the sort of thing he should treat with greatest suspicion. But as always he found himself ready to push boundaries and take chances. It was how he operated.

'Why didn't you say so?' he grunted casually, reaching for his hat.

Moran put a restraining hand on his arm. 'I'd be advisin' against it, Mr Stocker sir, indeed I would be.'

'You're hired help, not an adviser,' he said, shaking loose.

But the runty, bow-legged booze-hound followed as he made for the swinging doors.

'If you respond to · this female's invitation, then it's a fool you must be.'

Something about the man's expression caused Stocker to halt.

'Why? C'mon, spit it out man.'

'It's the commissioner's wife, damnit!'

Silence enshrouded the pair for a long moment. It didn't last, of course. Having tabbed his temporary sidekick as a drunk, a rogue and quite likely an Irish liar, Stocker's reaction was predictable.

'I told you to stay away from the booze, you — '

'It's the plain and honest truth I'm tellin' you, man. All shrouded up in black, so she is, but I seen her face and it's one that once seen never forgotten. And before that I was for seein' the big man's wife staring down from a window at the mansion when you were leavin' there . . . a flower-seller told me who she was.' He pointed. 'Now she's down here in the middle of the night with just a maid with her askin' to see you, of all people . . . '

'What do you mean by that?'

'Well, no offense, Mr Stocker, but you ain't exactly fitting company for any decent woman, are you now?'

'Go straight to hell.'

'Sir, just saying if your adventuring should sadly cost you your life. About the horse. Do you think you might just leave a note saying I might be the beneficiary?'

Chade dropped a curse and strode off towards the maw of the alley, hand on gunbutt, every sense alert. If this situation seemed strange to the Irishman it at least sounded highly suspect to him. Upon reaching the mouth, he removed his hat and peered round the corner. The shrouded shapes of two females stood outlined dimly by tallow light falling from a narrow window. A quick survey of the alley revealed no other sign of life.

Even so he hauled the Peacemaker before showing himself. He stood there silouetted against the glow of the plaza lights, gun cocked, finger taking the first pressure.

'Mr Stocker?'

'Who is it?'

'I think you know.'

He released the pressure on the trigger as he started forward. The voice was young, cultivated — the voice of an educated and possibly upper-class woman. As he approached, the taller of the two figures reached up and fingered back her hood in a graceful gesture. That dim light fell fully on her face and

Stocker heard his own sucked intake of breath. For once Moran hadn't exaggerated. She was beautiful.

She was plainly much younger than her husband, dark and pale with soft hair framing an oval face. She wore a golden silk scarf at her throat and kid gloves. She had quality stamped all over her and he was ready to accept her as Carrie Rackage, even without Irish Dave's affirmation.

And even before she'd opened her lips to speak again the gunman felt the treacherous, unbidden onset of that old familiar stirring.

He steeled himself against it. He knew his weaknesses but wasn't about to grant them breathing room here under the gibbous moon of the city. Couldn't afford the luxury.

'Mr Stocker?'

'At your service.'

'I've come to beg a favor.'

'Oh huh?'

'You have the look of a decent man — '

'I'm not. But I've been known to do a favor for a beautiful woman in my time.'

'Then, you consider me beautiful?'

Stocker was puzzled. There was nothing about this woman to suggest she was anything but the lady she had to be. Yet she seemed almost flirtatious with him, a total stranger and, by her standards, a dangerous man. Why should she bat dark eyelashes at him? Unless, of course, whatever it was she might want was so outrageous she felt it necessary to use whatever weapons she might possess.

He spoke sternly. 'What do you want?'

Carrie Rackage drew in a deep breath, gloved hands forming small fists.

'I want you to not kill Jesse McKidd.'

His jaw muscles worked, recalling he'd heard a whisper along the trail that there had once been something between the outlaw and the commissioner's wife. He'd thought it wildly unlikely on first hearing, felt even more strongly that way now, having met the lady. But the real irony of the situation was that she was asking of him the same thing which the commissioner had already virtually insisted, namely that McKidd be taken alive.

'So, you're that eager to see him do the rope dance too?'

'What on earth do you mean?'

Stocker clamped his lips. Seemed pretty plain that commissioner and lady did not exchange all confidences over the breakfast table if she didn't know Rackage meant to hang his man publicly as a warning to all. And staring down upon her smooth grave face, so pale against the black of her cowl, he felt strangely moved by her grace and sincerity, qualities which he rarely encountered in the breed of women he mixed with, yet could still recognize and admire.

He stepped back a pace. He removed his flat-brimmed hat and held it at his side. With his black glossy hair, powerful features and oiled bronze complexion, the gunman made an imposing figure as he stood motionless for a long handful of seconds, before nodding. He could sometimes be better than that. 'I won't kill him unless he makes me. That's the best I can do.'

'God bless you, Mr Stocker. I shall pray for you both.'

The women quit the alley by the far end. He heard a rig start up and wheel away, receding on rubber-tyred wheels. He didn't turn as by-now familiar shuffling steps approached warily from behind.

The Irishman's voice quivered with curiosity. 'By all the saints, man, and what did the beautiful creature be wantin' with the likes of you now . . . ?'

'Breathe one word of this and that breath'll be your last,' he growled, spinning on his heel and striding away.

He didn't want to talk. He wanted to think about her and what she had said. He was still a little dazed. Offhand he couldn't recollect any female, either good or bad, ever promising she would pray for him.

4

Man Against Boy

Territorians loved a good drama and what was being played out that summer against a backdrop of glittering deserts and mountains beneath the bleached-out skies of Canyon County, held the promise of being memorable, perhaps even legendary.

As one by one the posses, platoons, bountyhunter gangs and the ghoulish thrill-seekers dropped out of the fruitless hunt for Jesse McKidd, the fugitive dubbed killer by the law and the man named Stocker each began to loom larger in the public consciousness.

The scarred professional versus the young man who liked to dance the night away whenever he could give the law and his enemies the slip long enough to indulge himself — that proved a drama nobody seemed able to resist.

It seemed to have everything. And while many were rooting for McKidd there were equally as many who yearned for law and order to prevail. Such citizens found they could blind themselves to the McKidd mystique, and chose to regard Stocker, not as some kind of hired gun but rather as the commissioner's official appointee. These territorians therefore looked forward to an early arrest and trial in order that the doubts and confusion existing over the circumstances surrounding McKidd's crashout and the gun death of guard Roy Murch might finally be laid to rest.

Watching it all from the comfort and safety of the towns, it appeared to the valley citizens that McKidd appeared to be now drifting leisurely across the mighty landscapes of the county rather than running in fear. They noted the fugitive always appeared to be turning up for some anti-commissioner political rally, get-together or important occasion, either alone or with his bunch. He apparently felt unthreatened by either the bounty on his head or the menacing presence somewhere out there of a big man riding a palomino accompanied by an alcoholic Irishman who, or so it was now being rumored, might well be a horse thief of some notoriety known to the law in other parts of the territory.

However, the keen observer did note that McKidd appeared aware of the danger present now and was obviously smart enough to keep moving, never sleeping in the same spot twice.

Then there were the reports on McKidd's activities which were mysteriously supplied to the *Desert Denouncer* newspaper on a regular basis, and were subsequently published by that trusted organ.

It wasn't the first time the press had seemed to side with the administration's enemies, or had given wide space to McKidd.

The *Denouncer* had welcomed Rackage's appointment originally but had long since become disillusioned and often strident in its criticism of an administration which seemed to disregard the needs of the underdog while paving the way for the rich and powerful.

The paper had been among the first to identify the fact that McKidd's young hell-raisers had been amongst the commissioner's most severe critics from the outset, and therefore should be viewed as political enemies rather than outlaws. Soon, most everything they did in the way of fighting for some underdog or a lost cause was fully publicized in the pages of the *Denouncer*.

The editor freely conceded that a gang of wild riders scarcely shaped up as a worthy opposition to the established administration. But until some more credible faction appeared on the landscape, McKidd — murder warrant — would be the paper's symbol of the little man struggling for his rights.

The same paper was impartial enough to agree that Chade Stocker appeared more and more as authority's best prospect of success, this despite the obvious fact that he'd had no success in the manhunt thus far.

When sighted occasionally at watering holes, way stations, villages, forts and towns studded across Nogales Desert's limitless miles, Stocker always appeared confident and determined. Observers noted he appeared as indestructible as a chunk of desert granite and was rarely seen with his right hand more than a few inches away from gun handle, mute concession, so it would appear, to the caliber of the man he hunted.

Fortune, Havilland Wells, Mirage, Deep Junction, Gopherville, High Crest, Sundown and Outlaw Creek. A lot of towns and a lot of miles drifted behind in his dust over those weeks. But Stocker held to the trails and by late afternoon that searing day as they came down the trail toward Silver, he had a hunch he was closing in.

Irish Dave, worn down by the sheer relentlessness of the unending journey, was less optimistic as he rode along with chin on chest, rocking to his substitute mule's bone-jolting gait.

The horse-thief was so beat he'd all but stopped hatching his impossible scheme to get off with the palomino and gallop to Mexico City, which he reckoned would be none too far if he expected to outlast Stocker's pursuit.

He was restricted to what Stocker allowed him to drink while on the trail. In his liquor-denied fantasies he saw himself astride the palomino and riding with McKidd while murderously plotting Stocker's brutal assassination.

That day, he seemed to be raving again as the shimmering rooftops of yet another desert hell-hole showed ahead.

'I see the green!' he cried, throwing arms wide. 'A verdant green land, great green rivers . . . green skies. It's holy Mother Ireland and the girleens I'm seein' . . . the plump ones, the ones who smell of the flowers, the virgins and the married ones who know all the tricks and whose husbands are far away, whose loins ache with lust for a stallion of a man to come riding down the trail with nothing on his mind but their tender pale flesh, the golden thighs, the breasts so soft that to touch them is to know paradise . . . Don't you see them, you great oxblock of a man?'

Stocker rode on as though alone.

He was a rock. He knew exactly what the Irishman was about. Irish Dave wanted to spell up at Silver, maybe sit in a bath chair for a week and nurse his saddle blisters. So now the devious little runt was trying to lure him back down the crimson pathway of temptation.

It wouldn't work. Not this time.

They didn't find their man in Silver. But long hours spent sleuthing his way from bar to dive to rundown hotel, and after putting himself outside a lousy leathery steak and a totally first-class treble whiskey, Stocker finally did encounter the sage.

From the outset the gunman sensed the ancient Comanche half-breed had something on his mind when he approached him. And he was right.

'Good man, McKidd,' insisted the old shaman with the shoulder length gray pigtails and a nose like Geronimo's horse. 'He brave, he ride like Cochise and he fight like the Cheyenne at Sand Creek. He like brother, but even he should not show the disrespect. So say the sage.'

Stocker poured him a glass. 'Couldn't agree more,' he said easily. He sat and waited. Plainly this man wanted to talk. And eventually, in his own good time he finally came out with it.

'No paleface should ever visit the Old Ones of Shaman Canyon,' he stated unequivocally. 'Even blood brothers only welcome to the spirits when the medicine is right. I have spoken.'

It took an hour of patient interrogation and bribery before Stocker was satisfied he understood what the old

Indian meant. The Old Ones was the tribal name given to the ancient forebears of the desert Indians, the primitives who had once lived and thrived south-west of Silver in mysterious, haunted Shaman Canyon.

Stocker finally grasped the Indian was telling him that the man he was hunting may have disturbed the sacred dwelling place of the Old Ones.

Although the Irish horse thief protested passionately they were still far out along the south-west trail well before midnight.

★ ★ ★

The commissioner dined in style. The Harvard educated and West Point trained ex-soldier and career diplomat had always been accustomed to the better things in life and saw no reason to lower his standards simply because destiny had seen fit to dump him in possibly the harshest corner of the country.

Crystal, candles, immaculate linen and fine service characterized formal dinners at the old Spanish palace on the square ever since Rackage's inauguration. Tonight was no different. There might be any amount of tough talk and political wrangling around the big center table before the night was through, but style would be maintained until the last guest had departed.

The conversation flowed easily at first with the railroad tycoon revealing his plans for a new line — with the government's permission of course — while Mrs Rackage charmed everyone with her wit and quick intelligence.

The commissioner frequently interrupted what he was saying to beam proudly upon his young wife, and it was difficult for anyone present, even Rackage's political enemies, seeing them together this way, to give credence to those ugly rumors persisting in the wake of the upheaval of the whole McKidd affair.

Nobody seemed to know whether the

evil gossip linking Carrie Rackage and Jesse McKidd first leaked out before or after the wild boy's arrest and imprisonment in Capital City.

But then, as now, it received little credence amongst thinking citizens.

Gracious, cultivated Carrie Rackage and that wild scapegrace? Who could give credence to such a thing? It was so obvious that the Rackages doted upon one another. Plainly the whole thing was nothing more than a scurrilous story put about by the commissioner's enemies.

But the subject of McKidd was uppermost on the guests' minds tonight, and eventually, inevitably, someone posited the question.

'Commissioner, any fresh news from the manhunt?'

Rackage was halfway through his dessert of peaches and whipped cream at the time. His response was honest. Honesty in all matters had been his key pledge during the elections and not even his bitter political foe, liberal Jacob

Jacobs, could as yet catch him out in a lie.

'There's ample news but little of it encouraging, I'm afraid,' he confessed. 'As you're probably aware, virtually all the search parties have either given up or been recalled, leaving the matter at the moment in the hands of Mr Stocker. I'm satisfied he's pursuing his quarry with all vigor but thus far with little tangible success.'

Glances were exchanged, throats cleared. Upon Stocker's initial arrival in the capital little was known of him by the Bright's City man in the street. This no longer applied. In the wake of his appointment and the subsequent huge brawl involving him here in the city, the gunman had become a talking point and a subject of great interest.

By this, all Bright's City knew that the commissioner's appointee boasted a daunting reputation as a sometime government operative and enforcer. He was also known less flatteringly in other places as a womanizer, brawler and hellraiser, characteristics which the commissioner's enemies and critics liked to dwell upon at every opportunity.

So Rackage found himself defending his appointment yet again tonight, something he found less easy to do in light of the fact that, ten days on, McKidd was still very much at large with public sympathy for the young hellion plainly on the increase.

Could the commissioner afford this widely publicized manhunt to continue much longer without running the risk of his administration being made appear weak and ineffectual?

This question was eventually put by the opposition leader who'd run against Rackage in the bitterly contested election, Jacob Jacobs, himself.

'The matter is well in hand, Jacobs,' Rackage assured blandly, leading the guests to the drawing room.

'What if McKidd should flee the country?'

'Then that would solve our problem, wouldn't it?'

'But would it solve the problem of the damaging talk, Commissioner?'

Jacobs said this with a direct look at the commissioner's wife. Everyone was silent for a long moment. Then the three-piece band struck up and Rackage took Carrie in his arms to dance.

'Talk, as you should realize as one of the most renowned talkers as opposed to achievers in this territory, Mr Jacobs,' he said in a voice that carried, 'doesn't boil beans. Do please stop carrying the burdens of my concerns on your shoulders and try and enjoy yourself. I'm told your lady wife complains that you haven't danced with her since your wedding night twenty years ago.'

Some sniggered, some actually laughed out loud. Jacobs's fleshy face burned. He'd been bested and knew it. And circling the floor with his smiling wife in his arms as the band played, the county commissioner looked like a man without a real care in the world. 'I love you, darling,' he told his wife.

But dark-haired Carrie seemed not to hear.

* * *

People liked to gather on the benches around the fountain down on the square whenever the commissioner entertained. The high windows of the palace were flung open on summer nights and the sounds of the string trio wafting down and the occasional glimpse of elegantly dressed figures drifting by the doorways conjured up images of style and refinement such as many a towner never got to see.

It also provided a good opportunity for the sit-and-spit factions, the character assassins and the plain jawbone gossips to get together and catch up on the latest.

There was talk of land rights, railroad, cattle prices, outlawry in the south, and of course, still the topic of the day, the hunt for Jesse McKidd, the man the commissioner still vowed would eventually swing.

It wasn't until he heard McKidd's name through an alcoholic haze that town lush Drunky John stirred on his plank bench, waved his brown bottle and made his booming bass-drum voice heard.

'Never done it,' he proclaimed. 'Might've stole Barney Tebbs's cow that night, could easy have been the feller what shinnied up Cole Madison's drainpipe and painted slogans all over his barn roof. Ain't sayin' he never. What I am sayin' is that whatever else he coulda done, Jesse never gunned down Roy Murch. No way, nohow, not never.'

'Sure, Drunky, sure,' a bystander said patronizingly. 'You know on account you was there, right?'

'I sure as hell was.'

'Yeah, like you was there at the signin' of the peace at Appomattox, and in the box the night Lincoln was assassinated.'

People laughed as the drunk staggered to his feet. 'I seen it happen,' he insisted, gesticulating. 'True as I'm standin' here. Tall feller wearin' a long black cape, silver pistol . . . seen him clearly as I'm seein' you.'

'In other words — none too clearly, eh, Drunky boy?'

Derisive applause marked the weaving figure's haughty retreat. Somehow Drunky John's little performance seemed to strike the right foolish note on what, by and large, was turning out to be a pretty pleasant and unusually untroubled night in the county capital.

★   ★   ★

All afternoon the country had been growing rougher, sliding away from desert into badlands. Growth was scarcer, lizards and chuckwallers scuttled away at the sound of horses, raising tiny puffs of red dust. It was dry, bad country that made a man tetchy.

Stocker reined in to take off his hat and swab his brow. As he did, something rustled in deep brush close by, something heavy. He twisted in the saddle, hand going to Colt in a lightning draw. He whipped out the piece, cocking and extending it to arm's length in one fluent motion, touching off two explosive rounds so fast they sounded as one big blast of sound.

Echo chased echo off down the mouth of a raddled canyon as they waited, a grimacing Irish Dave hauling his sombrero down around his ears, Stocker a graven image with his finger on the trigger, eyes cut to a single steely gleam focused on the brush clump.

Stocker stared through swirling powder smoke. Then he swung down and advanced on the thicket. Something rustled in the brush. He extended the .45 ready to fire again, then lowered the cutter with a grunt.

'What?' Moran's voice trembled. The deeper they had cut into the canyon-cut badlands the more jittery he'd become. Terrain didn't disturb the Irishman but he was vulnerable to spooky legends. 'Is it the ghost?'

Stocker leaned forward and hauled the small, quivering body out of the brush. Both slugs had slammed into the javalina's body. He dropped the animal and walked back down the slope.

'Just keeping my hand in,' he said, swinging up.

'No, begorrah, it's more than that. I can be tellin' you can feel the evil here just like meself. It's time we faced the facts and turned and left, Stocker. This place is bedevilled, fer sure. Not even a young feller they claim fears nothin' on earth would stick his snout in this benighted place.'

Stocker felt his frown cut deep. He was aware that the farther they travelled without sight of their quarry, the more testy he became with remarks even vaguely flattering of the elusive McKidd.

'Wrong. Very place he would look for. We'll push on. It'll be dark soon and there's weather comin'.'

That was just what Irish Dave didn't want to hear, darkness and bad weather to add the final touch to what was shaping up as one of the worst journeys of his life.

'This be the land of the dead.'

'Move that jackass along.'

'You have no respect for the dead.'

'Or jittery drunks. Keep up, Irishman, or get left behind.'

'Faith, you don't even know if these tracks we're followin' belong to that damned spalpeen kid.'

'They're his.'

'Maybe you're right. I sense eyes upon us now.'

'I should have brought some garlic.'

This remark was puzzling enough to draw Moran's attention from their forbidding surrounds.

'Garlic?'

'They wear it to frighten off spooks and vampires.' Stocker glanced over his shoulder. 'The old women and scaredy little kids, back where I come from, that is.' His black stare bored hard as a rock drill. 'Keep up or I'll leave you behind.'

Dave Moran was sufficiently offended

to lapse into a sullen silence. But he wasn't insulted enough not to bring his cayuse in close to the palomino's hindquarters for security. He shivered even though the storm hadn't reached them yet. This was one scared Irishman who stared at Stocker's back with total hatred.

Stocker simply concentrated on the sign.

McKidd's trail, which he'd picked up several miles outside Silver, could be read with ease. The fugitive rode a horse with a long stride and distinctively shaped hoofs which angled slightly outwards. It was said to be a magnificent animal which the outlaw had won in a poker game. Stocker wouldn't know about that, only knew it was a big strong horse, well ridden and cared for. And that it was still travelling steadily west.

He saw where McKidd cantered, when he walked or trotted, when he took a drink, swerved to avoid a rattler, or halted to feed his mount from his saddlebags on grass and corn nubbins.

His mental image of McKidd in the desert seemed to grow plainer with every mile. Lithe, quick moving, superb trailsman, easy on his mount, not prone to making errors of judgment.

Impressive.

Stocker grimaced. He'd listened to any amount of bullshit about McKidd during the hunt, wanted to avoid building him up too tall in his mind now he sensed they could be getting close. On the other hand, he could not afford to underestimate the man. You could die just as easy underrating someone as building them up so big in your mind it frayed your nerve and sapped your confidence.

The composite picture he'd fashioned of his quarry was that of a man too young to be as good as he was, faster than most, gutsy enough — and with more friends than a politician passing a free beer bill.

And a big head?

He hoped so. That could prove his

Achilles. And Chade Stocker would never admit to anyone that in light of what he now knew, guessed and had learned about the man, he might need all the advantages he could muster when they came face to face again.

He hipped about to see Irish Dave hunched miserably in the saddle. He could imagine what it might do to the Irishman's spirit were he to concede that, even should they track their man down out here, that might not be the end of it, that it could prove a touch-and-go showdown. Moran's alcoholic heart might crack like an old walnut.

Brown birds pecked at a pile of horse droppings. Small critters ran beneath clumps of manzanita. The sun was swinging low and thunderheads were building behind the mesas.

Stocker halted. The smell of horse came to him on the wind. The breeze was sharper and blowing stronger.

Somewhere a hoof struck stone.

'Yonder!' he hissed, indicating a

brushy draw off to the right. They had barely taken cover when the Indian woman appeared. She was gray and stooped, sitting in the crude saddle strapped to the bony ribcage of a Roman-nosed pony with burrs in its tail.

Stocker pushed the palomino out to block her way, raised his hand in greeting. She stared at them dully, unsurprised but vaguely disgusted.

'Hau.'

Her voice was deep and hoarse.

'You see Jesse McKidd?' Stocker demanded.

'Yes.'

'Where?'

'He sleeps with the Old Ones, he will not waken.'

'I want to know where — '

'Nor shall you waken, White Eyes,' the old woman cut in harshly. 'I tend the sleeping ones and they are restless, angered by the intruders. Even I who love them leave in fear.' She gestured at the turbulent elements. 'On such nights they may rise and paint their faces and walk amongst their enemies and those who defile their resting place. The outlaw's naked bones will greet the dawn, as will your own . . . '

She was gone, fading into the misting rain that was the precursor of what was coming.

'For God's sake, Stocker, if that warnin' ain't enough to — '

'Don't start.'

He pushed on purposefully, heeling the palomino through a screen of brush then along a narrow gully track and over a rise to see the whole country gape and yawn directly before him. Shaman's Canyon.

He looked over his shoulder. Irish Dave Moran was now no place to be seen as the first jagged bolt of staghorn lightning daubed the landscape eerie blue.

5

Ghost Guns

Stocker stashed the golden palomino in a draw where an overhang of yellow stone shielded it from the worst of the rain.

Slicker flapping, his cigar a cherry red blob in the dark of his face, he slung the Winchester over his shoulder and began to walk.

The box canyon was enormous here, high-walled and echoing, a surreal landscape of rotting vegetation, petrified trees and giant, broken boulders. The lightning came so constantly that soon he didn't even bother to pause before continuing on. The stream was already running, would quickly deepen if the storm kept dumping its icy loads out of a blackened sky.

The stone monuments were his first

warning that he was coming to something. He checked the manmade pillars out warily; they would make excellent cover for a dry-gulcher.

There were no tracks here with all signs sluiced away by the rain which was now whistling down-canyon at an almost horizontal plane, cutting at his skin, his eyes.

He spat rain water and kept walking. Storms didn't bother him, old monuments held no fears. But he was anything but relaxed. Had his quarry spent a week setting up the perfect ambush site in the most advantageous conditions, he couldn't have done better.

Thunder drums rumbled in his ears as the manhunter pushed himself up a slope that was running with braided streams of surface water. The rain hammered off his hatbrim and sluiced off his slickered shoulders. Now he walked for a time in total darkness as the lightning slacked off. Then it suddenly crackled back into life with stunning brilliance, and in the vivid illumination he gazed up to see the lofted stone vaults he'd been told about and knew he had reached the ancient Yuma lodge and burial site.

Tier upon tier, the ancient man-made galleries rose and Stocker was hard put to maintain his indifference at the spectacle of what had been a thriving, primitive city long before Columbus raised the East Coast centuries before.

You could feel the strangeness in the air; he couldn't deny it. Certainly lightning and lashing rain and the awareness that someone could be staring down at him over a set of gunsights hardly provided a calm and detached atmosphere. But there was something here, something intangible but undeniable, and he had to wonder for a moment if maybe the Irishman hadn't been the smart one, taking off as he'd done . . .

He shook the thought away, jacked a shell into his Winchester, waited.

He knew there had been no sign of life up on the highest level when that first brilliant burst of lightning brought the whole ghostly edifice into sharpened relief.

Yet now as shimmering blue light again flooded the ghostly chambers and ancient storm voices rumbled in subterranean regions beneath his boots, there stood above him a figure, motionless, rimmed in the lightning's shimmer, staring down.

Then it was gone.

He licked his lips. Funny, but when he agreed to take on Rackage's manhunt he'd thought in practical terms: gun punk, routine chase, dangerous doubtless but in essence a pretty routine job of work like he'd handled many times before.

He'd never envisioned finding himself one-out in a storm-lashed canyon from the past in the middle of an evil night battling the bad medicine notion and wondering if maybe his eyes weren't playing him tricks when blackness fell like a club, then sprang alight under the lightning — and the high tier was empty.

He squared his shoulders. Earn your money, Stocker. They can't all be pushovers.

Taking stock of his surrounds, he picked out a staircase hewn out of the cliff face forming the southern wall of the great vault.

Moments later he was climbing slowly, hugging the walls, clinging to the shadows, a heavy shouldered silhouette in streaming yellow slicker, hatbrim tugged low over slitted eyes, the complete huntsman.

He counted four stone levels before it happened.

The shot rang out with shocking suddenness, its impact magnified by the walls of the mighty chamber, the whine of the ricochet harrying the eardrums like the whining bits of a whipsaw on steel.

He dropped flat, amazed to realize he'd not been hit.

Then the voice: 'Begone, intruder of the sacred place!'

Stocker rolled beneath the mantel of a doorway. 'Shove it, killer!'

A soft laugh floated down the stairwell.

'Didn't think you'd swallow the hoopla, big man. Still, it was worth a try. Only thing, now I'll likely have to kill you.'

'I don't fancy your chances, punk!' Stocker's tone was harsh and confident. But he was forcing it. He knew he'd just averted death by a whisker. No matter how often that happened a man never developed immunity to the fear of it. 'You had your chance and you fouled up.'

'I had you cold.'

'Then why am I still breathing?'

'On account that was just a warning shot, big man.'

'Sure.' Stocker was straining his eyes, twisting his big head this way and that when the lightning came. But all he saw were criss-crossing networks of stone parapets and ramparts reaching high into that roiling sky. 'Like the warnin' shot you put into that deputy in Bright's.'

'I didn't shoot Murch. But I sure could have killed you just now, hardnose.'

'Tell me — '

'Feel your hatbrim, left side.'

Stocker raised his hand. His fingers found the bullet hole immediately. He cursed softly.

'You've gone quiet, Stocker.'

Stocker whirled, hands brushing the metal surfaces of his rifle as he squinted upwards. By now he had a rough notion where the other was located but drew little comfort from the knowledge. He was pinned down. He was a good ten feet from the stairs he'd climbed. He had cover here, sure, but it was severely limited and he would be exposed were he to move one more full step,

More points to the killer. He'd lured him here, now had the drop on him. Good one, Stocker.

'You're out of your depth, McKidd! I'm older and uglier and about ten times smarter than you. You've had half a thousand men lookin' for you but I'm the one who found you. Why do you think they hired me if they didn't know I could deliver. The best I can offer you is, throw down your irons and I'll take you in alive. You've got my word on that.'

There was the sound of boot leather scraping against stone, a sigh.

'I believe you, Stocker. Know why? On account I know all about Rackage braggin' to the whole blue-eyed territory on how he's aimin' to try me and swing me right there on the square in Bright's to make sure no dumb heads mistake me for any kind of hero anymore. Ain't that how it is bein' played?'

'He could have told me to fetch you in feet first.'

'I'm no hero, man. But neither is he. The commissioner ain't what he seems.'

'How about the commissioner's wife, punk?'

'Guess it's no good talkin' to a man like you, is it? You're all out of the same mold, and a pretty crummy mold it is too.'

'You should know all about crummy, kid.' Stocker was sweating, eyes continuing to play restlessly every which way, searching desperately for anything that might suggest a way out of this bind.

Turned out he didn't need it.

'Ok, big man,' now McKidd's voice sounded tired, resigned. 'I can see I've been wasting my time tryin' to talk to you. Let's do it.'

'What?'

'Shoot it out of course — you lousy, stinking hired gun son of a whore! Show your ass and we'll play the game by the rules, and I'll put you out of your misery. Let's duel it up, big man.'

Stocker was stunned. This was the last thing he'd expected. But maybe he shouldn't be surprised. The man had out-drawn him once. Then again, it could be a trap. Yet somehow he didn't believe that. Maybe, after all, McKidd was nothing but a cocky little gun punk ready to put his life on the line to prove he was number one, a kid's game Stocker had given away years before.

'You reckon you've got my number then, eh, kid?'

'Do you want to fight or knit bed socks?'

Stocker rose to one knee.

'You show yourself first, McKidd!'

'Don't play games, big man.' The young gun's voice was thin with worn-out patience. 'I'm coming out now and you better do the same, rememberin' I can see you but you can't see me.'

'But — '

'Now, you bastard, now!'

The slim figure appeared in full sight, head tilted downwards, empty hands hanging by his side. The spectacle struck a primitive response in the gunman touching off vivid memories of his young days when he, like the kid, was flamboyant and recklessly earning the Colt chevrons which he now wore with such assurance.

Now he was standing. Their eyes met and locked through thirty feet of swirling air.

'Thunderclap, punk!'

'Thunderclap it is, big man.'

It came quickly, a deep booming sound like God clearing his throat. Stocker lunged forward and went into his draw in unison with the man above. Two swift hands slapped steel together — then both froze.

Stocker's six-shooter sights were framed squarely on the chest of McKidd whose own shooter had barely cleared its cutaway holster.

For a moment the tableau held, the glitter in Stocker's black eyes mirroring triumph while the last ounce of color drained from the young gun's face.

The score was now even. And Stocker was ready to squeeze the trigger and kill his man where he stood if he moved a muscle, when he felt movement beneath his right boot where he'd lunged forward going into the draw. He'd stamped down on what he took to be a solid petrified deadfall. But the gray formation was hollow and his weight was too much.

He was falling. He squeezed off a shot but knew he'd missed as he plunged down. His shot was answered by another and fire lanced through his right flank.

The tomb of the Old Ones shuddered with the thunder then trembled to the gun blasts until the whole teetering vault of stone seemed to shiver on its ancient foundations before the falling Stocker's head struck stone and he pitched, plunging into blackness as deep as the grave.

★   ★   ★

They had stretched him out on a big iron griddle and horned devils stoked up the fires beneath until he was well broiled on one side and it was time to turn him over.

Then he awoke.

His first sensation was one of disbelief to find himself still alive. His brain felt like something encased in thick cotton wool and he couldn't see straight, yet the sudden jolt of pain was an agonizing but welcome reminder that he was indeed alive, yet surely had no right to be.

The gun battle was real.

He'd out-drawn the kid but his footing giving way had cost him his lightning advantage. He'd gotten two shots away. Had he seen the kid buckle or was that just wishful thinking? But the kid had had him cold on that final shot — so how come he was still alive?

The flare of the killer's last shot had been as real and vivid as anything he'd ever seen. So how come, at that range, he wasn't dead?

He groaned and rolled over. It was a mistake. Somehow during his long hours of unconsciousness, he must have moved to the stone stairwell. He went over, thudding down riser after riser, each impact sending a jolt of pure white agony through his ribs.

It was almost pleasurable to drop onto a broad stone landing with a solid dead-meat thud and know he couldn't fall any farther.

Stocker lay in blazing sunshine. He was stretched out on his back and there was a salt taste in his mouth. He wanted to move again but his cottonwool brain was now operating just well enough to make a suggestion. Take inventory first, both of his condition and his position. He didn't know how badly he was hurt but was rock solid certain he wouldn't survive another drop down the stairwell.

The bullet had caught him in the lower ribs on the right-hand side.

His fingers began to explore, moving over barrel chest, muscular mid section, lower. His shirt was caked in dried blood but he could not find any further bullet holes, no broken bones as far as he could judge.

He hurt, sure he hurt. But if it came

down to cases he knew he was more mystified than suffering.

Why?

It had been one-against-one and the laurel wreath of victory went to Jesse McKidd. Again. He'd beaten the punk to the draw yet when he lost his footing he ended up the one with a bullet in him. One bullet. The man had downed him but didn't finish him off. He suspected he might have given the other six in the guts had their positions been reversed.

Maybe something had distracted the killer? He grimaced. Sure, something like a ghost.

Opening his eyes, he forced himself up on one elbow. He was in bad shape, shot up, abandoned most likely, left to die. Yet alive. The word had never sounded quite so fine. He grunted as he forced himself up onto one knee and knelt there until the vault of the Old Ones stopped spinning.

He was up.

Warily placing one foot ahead of the

other he began to descend. He found it hard to believe he'd climbed so high. No sign of life, nothing but hot patches of sunlight on burning rock offset by pits of black shadow.

No ghosts.

He felt free to admit now that last night, seeing this place for the first time and with the storm raging and flashing to provide the perfect atmosphere, he'd found Shaman's Canyon a pretty grim place to be.

Today it was almost sylvan under this typical territory sun, almost beautiful. Somehow . . . light-headed maybe . . . he seemed to feel a twinge of regret that he and the kid had felt obliged to bring their brutal business here.

Already his tongue was furring and thick. His whole body was dried out and he'd give his right arm for a double shot.

But his troubles were just beginning.

The rocky alcove where he'd stashed the palomino was empty. There was water here in the canyon but nothing beyond for — how many miles?

Ripping out a shirtsleeve he strapped up his chest as best he could and lighted up. He was grateful for tobacco. He might forgive a man for drilling him to the draw and leaving him for dead then stealing his horse, but surely his adversary had proven himself not to be a total bastard by leaving him his makings.

Adios to the Old Ones.

Setting off east along the canyon floor he soon left the vaults behind to follow the course of the canyon stream through thornbrush, talus and drooping sycamore. He marched to the beat of a steady drum, and the drumbeat was the pounding in his head.

It was simply the instinct for self-preservation that got him started, but after an hour of sun, thirst and pain it was willpower that took over.

Stocker had always had determination to burn. He knew he could last an hour, maybe a day. But how far was it

133

back to Silver anyway? The closest he could figure was — one hell of a long way. But he knew he could make it. Keep the mind blank and the legs going forwards. Nothing to it.

Halfway to sundown found him reeling a little but still driving forward, a big shambling man in a bloodstained shirt, jaw unshaven, red-rimmed eyes fixed on the middle distance ahead, riding boots slowly coming apart from the bite of gravel and stone, yet continuing on, deliberate as destiny and only dimly aware of his surroundings until he heard his horse.

He dived behind a tree and filled his hand with sixgun. There was a brief moral dilemma. If it proved to be McKidd coming back down-canyon, would he give him a chance to surrender considering his having spared his life? Or would he gun him down?

Gun him down, of course. This was no game of chivalry even if the gun punk might think otherwise.

The horse sounded again. Only then

he realized it was not a horse at all, but a jackass.

A jackass?

He cocked his cutter and scrunched lower as movement showed through the brush and moments later the Irish drunk hove into sight, jogging to the animal's rough gait, hat flopping and eyes rolling left and right, as fearful as a virgin in a whorehouse.

Dirty son of a —

Stocker bit down on his temper and forced himself to relax. He was leaning almost nonchalantly against his tree when the rider cleared the brush and sighted him.

'All the holy saints of Ireland be praised! It's a blessed miracle. Welcome back to the land of the livin', me boyo!'

Stocker's expression did not change. It was granite to begin with and so remained.

Moran grew aware of this only after flinging himself off the animal's broad back and starting forwards at the run. Now he propped with uncertainty clouding his features.

'Amigo?'

Stocker cocked his Colt and the man jumped a foot.

'Ahh, me good friend, I see you've been injured and in need of assistance.' A forced grin. 'Sure and it's fortunate beyond belief that after I strayed from the trail I finally found me bearings again and set out to find you, wouldn't you be agreein'?'

This was pure bullshit and Stocker recognized it as such. Long before the showdown, this man had quit on him. Left him, as it eventuated, to come within an ace of being killed. What vaguely puzzled him as he thrust the other from his path and attacked canteen and saddlebags, was why the yellow horse thief had returned now instead of finding a nice safe bed back in Silver to crawl under.

They weren't together an hour before Moran began making veiled references to Stocker's palomino, references which became more frequent and overt over

136

the miles until it slipped out, until the man couldn't help revealing he'd met the ancient Indian woman again who had apparently rambled on about 'the big one's beautiful horse'.

Until Stocker understood.

Moran's return was not motivated by loyalty and concern but stemmed solely from his passion for his horse.

Served him right that the sign he'd read back at the canyon told him the horse had been taken by the man who shot him.

A grim Stocker felt almost relieved now that he understood. It meant he would not now have to thank Moran for possibly saving his life. He hated thanking people. He only wished he could figure out a way not to feel grateful to Jesse McKidd for not finishing him off when he had the chance.

6

The Takers

The desert lands were still.

Across the shimmering reaches where Apache, Pima, Comanche and Yaqui once roamed and ruled, today all was empty silence.

And yet despite this vast stillness coming as it did in the wake of weeks of frenzied activity surrounding the manhunt for Jesse McKidd, the winds of change, so long a part of Southwest Territory, were blowing more strongly on the day of Stocker's return to the capital than had been the case in years.

The word was out that the commissioner's hired gun had been met, bested and packed off home with his tail between his legs and a bullet in his ribs. That he'd even had horse and rifle taken from him.

Defeat and humiliation — with the kid's signature seal stamped on it for all to see.

Nothing could have stirred the city more that day. The fence-sitters of yesterday who'd been content to stand back and watch McKidd dealt with by any means the authorities deemed fit, today were having the bartenders top up their shot glasses while they ponderously debated whether maybe this headline-grabbing showdown out at Shaman's Canyon had been meant to happen. The hired gun had run the boy down on Rackage's orders, but McKidd had bested him then spared his life.

Was this a sign of some kind to force them to see McKidd in a different light and ponder the revived big question: what if the kid was not the black villain the commissioner had been painting him? And when that question was asked it opened the gates once again on all the contentions that had cast Rackage in the role of the underhanded power-grabber and McKidd the little man's only strong friend.

Only McKidd could create such fervent interest or whip up emotions strong enough to stir again the winds of unrest, which Rackage had been fighting to quell.

The reason McKidd could create such response, divide communities so strongly and set friend against friend and brother against brother, was simplicity itself. In a harsh land of few genuine heroes, he was, or had been, the real thing.

The only son of a famed frontiersman, wagon master and visionary, McKidd seemed to have had it all from the outset, excelling at virtually every benchmark by which Westerners judged themselves. Horseman, marksman, bon vivant, charmer, fighter, lover and friend, he was every territorian's favorite son, brother, sweetheart or best pard.

Of course, the one incident that had

set the seal on the man's renown and popularity had been the Adobe Creek incident last year. At that stage the administration attempted to shift on a clan of Mexicans who'd farmed the creek valley for generations in order to open it up to migrant settlement. McKidd and his partners had leapt to the Mexicans' defence, had garnered wide support from others and in the end had forced Rackage to back off.

Things like that, along with the fact that he appeared to have so many gifts, yet seemed devoid of vanity or arrogance or weakness had in time cemented his position as the county's favorite son.

This was the purely honorary and unofficial ranking, yet was very real, almost tangible, indeed it seemed he may have gone on living his wild free life with the boys as he'd always done, roaming, hunting, helping out friends in the occasional range war or rustler troubles, freewheeling through life, never showing really serious for more

141

than five minutes at a stretch — but for the killing.

The arrest, crashout and killing of the deputy in the capital had aroused the desert regions in a way which seemed disproportionate to its actual significance.

And now, as the Jacobeans fulminated against the commissioner's incompetence and with Rackage putting in twelve-hour days at his palace office and looking more drawn and harassed by the day, plus the report that big Stocker was confined to his sick bed at the Pawnee Hotel off the square, even the capital's dogs seemed to be barking unrest, uncertainty and brewing trouble.

While Rackage himself was at the moment being hailed as guest of honor out at the Tiptoe ranch where the owner, one of the richest men in the territory, was publicly warning the commissioner to initiate an immediate high-level judicial inquiry into the entire McKidd affair, or be prepared to accept the consequences.

It was common knowledge that Tiptoe's van Goodeve was a fellow Cattleman's Club member along with Jacob Jacobs, and was reported to have recently entertained hard-nosed General Kirk, prime contender for the role of military administrator should congress return Southwest Territory to the bad old days of martial law.

Rumor had it that Rackage's support base was beginning to crumble, and it did seem more and more evident that some of his strongest supporters were beginning to lose faith in his leadership.

There was an old western expression that if something strange was going to happen any place it would most likely happen in Southwest Territory. If an administration's very existence could be threatened by the events surrounding one turbulent kid, then it would seem that this old saying might be proven out in a way hitherto never seen before.

* ★ ★

He made a bad patient.

'Nobody's washing me but me,' he growled from the big four-poster in Room 22. 'And get that goddamn peep-show gallery out of this room before I get up and throw them out. And I'm bird naked under this sheet in case you don't know it, sister woman.'

But shapely Marta simply smiled tolerantly as she entered the room toting a pail of steaming water. She was young and buxom and smiled all the time, simply refusing to take his bad temper and tantrums seriously. He might have actually thrown her out had she been less attractive, or if he were capable of tossing anybody out of any place, the shape he was in.

He just wanted to be alone to lick his wounds like an animal until he was back to full strength and fit to resume the task assigned to him:

Get the kid.

Nothing had really changed from his point of view. He might be aware that there had been huge support for McKidd in the week following the canyon shootout, but he was indifferent to that. He'd suffered a setback, not defeat. He was still on the commissioner's payroll and never quit a job unfinished.

The maid began washing him, or at least what she could get at, his upper chest, shoulders and arms, his lower torso being encased in clean white strapping.

Too disgusted even to curse, Stocker slumped back against his plumped-up pillows and stared balefully at his audience.

They sat on straight-backed chairs across the room, Marta's motley assembly of relations, ranging from a fifteen-year-old kid in pigtails through a middle-aged woman who smoked a briar pipe, and an old maid wearing pince-nez.

Marta was so proud to have been

given the job of nursing the 'famous' Señor Stocker that after forty-eight hours she'd given into family pressure and brought her kinfolk along to see for themselves just what a renowned, even notorious individual looked like in the flesh.

He was loath to admit it, but he was almost pleased to glance up finally and see the familiar face peering round the doorway. His enjoyment didn't last long, however. After greeting him and his cheer squad, the Irishman presented the copy of the *Desert Denouncer*, hot off the press. The 48 point headline shouted:

McKIDD MERCIFUL IN VICTORY

The accompanying editorial went on to declare that the Rackage administration, was now under unprecedented pressure in the aftermath of Stocker's 'failure'. Moran seemed happy to report that at that very moment, General Kirk was staging an impromptu military parade through the city as if to remind the county that it still had the option of solid, reliable military rule should it decide it had had enough maladministration of the Rackage stamp.

'So, did you find it?' Stocker interrupted.

'Huh?'

'You know what I mean.'

The Irishman was puzzled, but Marta, busily brushing the patient's thick mane of black hair, was sharper.

'The señor believes you returned to the canyon only in the hope of retrieving his horse after he was shot, señor.'

Irish Dave looked shocked. For back out in the desert, a semi-conscious Stocker had levelled that same evil accusation against him. Moran had overlooked the insult and returned the injured gunman back to the capital. He couldn't believe any man could still be so suspicious and ungrateful.

He was on the verge of storming from the room when Stocker relented.

'OK, you're a hero. But my horse is still missing?'

Immediately appeased, Dave smiled. 'Still, I fear. Ahh . . . do you be planning to go after the wonderful animal when you're on your feet, old friend?'

'Get out!'

The Irishman just shrugged and rose from his chair. No matter how hard he tried to conceal his real intentions at times, whenever that lusted-after horse was involved he was transparent as window glass.

He was ready to leave but not before he'd discharged all his responsibilities.

'The commissioner's man, Clutter-loe,' he said stiffly, making for the door, 'said he will visit — '

'Tell him not to bother.'

'The commissioner sends his sympathies.'

'Tell him to send money.'

'The señorita who dances at the Two Bits Saloon says to tell you she believes McKidd ambushed you, but didn't beat you fair.'

'She does?' Stocker was touched. As far as he could determine from this lousy room most everybody else believed the young gun had bested him then had gallantly let him live. The fact that this had to be pretty close to the truth didn't comfort him any.

Irish Dave disappeared leaving Stocker doing a slow burn. Forty-eight hours, he calculated. That's how long it would take before he walked from this room, rented a good horse and rode out to finish what he'd started at Shaman's Canyon, not one minute more.

One thought strengthened him. He'd outdrawn that wild kid this time. He could do it again.

He must have dozed.

He awoke to realize Marta was massaging him. He hadn't asked for this. He was ready to growl at her, then realized it was kind of nice, arousing almost.

He looked at her sharply. She smiled warmly. There were tiny drops of perspiration between her big firm breasts. Stocker was soaking it up when knuckles hit the door, which opened to admit Bob Clutterloe flanked by Sergeant Bourke.

'Out!' The commissioner's man ordered the girl. He dropped big hands on the brass bed end as they left, the soldier folding his arms. 'You don't look too sick to me,' he remarked.

There was nothing subtle about Clutterloe. If he thought he had you at a disadvantage he didn't hesitate playing to it.

'I'll live,' Stocker said. 'What do you want?'

'The commissioner wants to know if you're all washed up,' Bourke supplied.

'Tell him thanks for his concern.'

'Skip the sarcasm, man,' warned Clutterloe. 'We're playing for big marbles here, just in case you don't realize it. The commissioner wagered big on you and you fouled up. I mean, really fouled up. That killer's still at large and we've got the dogs baying for a public inquiry, thanks to you. What we need to know is — '

'I've got two things to say,' Stocker cut in, steely-eyed. 'One, I'll be riding Thursday and won't be coming back without his man. The second? I don't want to pick up any germs hindering my recovery, so maybe if you're all through . . . ?'

An angry Clutterloe stared at Bourke, who moved threateningly towards the bed. Stocker's big gun lay on the bedside table within reach. He picked up the weapon and trained it on Bourke's chest. Bourke stumbled backwards and Clutterloe gaped in shock as Stocker deliberately cocked the piece with a well-oiled click. He grinned for the first time since the shootout as two shocked officials high tailed, leaving the door wide open.

He settled back against his pillows. It seemed the incident had done him more good than a whole pint of Doc Hudson's medicine. Maybe he might even be fit enough to ride come Wednesday? He closed his eyes and concentrated on figuring out how he would find McKidd.

It was no longer just a job. This was personal.

★ ★ ★

The bright green paintwork of the Titan locomotive glistened through billowing clouds of steam, smoke and hoof-lifted dust as the bridge showed half a mile ahead.

'You're gonna lose your wager, Jesse!' laughed the sweating fireman, leaning from the footplate to wave his cap derisively at the horsemen riding all out to overtake the first car. 'A hundred horses'll whip five any day of the week!'

'This ain't any day — this is *the* day, you broken-winded old hammerhead!' shouted McKidd, racing the golden palomino ahead of his companions now. 'First to the bridge, a hundred bucks. Double if you want.'

As engineer and fireman conferred

above the slam of pistons and whistling slipstream, some forty-odd passengers sat rigid in their seats with fear while a young bunch hooted and howled and urged their crewmen to greater effort as the Saint Simon bridge loomed ahead and McKidd's galloping horse gained ground, now hammering along the flank of the swaying coal tender.

The 'infamous' McKidd gang was back to doing what they did best — having one hell of a fine time.

The crewmen could lose their jobs, yet doubted they would. The A & W boss played poker in Bright's City, had often played with McKidd, or had done before the jailbreak.

So they gave the Titan all it had over that last half-mile, only to grind their teeth in chagrin as the palomino, pounding along the right-of-way, slowly but surely overtook the locomotive to the cheers of the other riders and the wails of the passengers, who, leaning from their windows, could see their bets going down the drain.

But even as he drew ahead, McKidd didn't let up. The contrary. He was coaxing the last ounce out of his champion cayuse, and the bridge was less than a hundred yards ahead before redheaded Clay realized what he had in mind.

'No, Jesse!' he bawled. 'Don't be crazy!'

Too late. Drawing three horse-lengths ahead of the loco, McKidd suddenly jerked hard on his right-hand rein. To wide-eyed riders and ashen-faced passengers it seemed as the palomino disappeared in front of the engine that it must be struck. Then the train was storming onto the bridge, and on the right-hand side, sitting the saddle of his rearing bronc and waving his Stetson was McKidd, unscathed and laughing to kill.

The 4.10 to Bright's City was gone and four young men sat their saddles staring at the fifth in awe.

'That was loco, Jesse,' said Enoch, shaking his head. 'We'd already won the wager. Why stick your neck out that way?'

◆'Why not, amigo?' he laughed, leading them off across the desert at the lope. 'Give me one good reason why not?'

They shook their heads and looked at one another as they trailed through his dust, and none could see his face now. McKidd wasn't smiling any longer. Usually this kind of caper was prompted by sheer high spirits and a sense of daring, his way of dealing with the greatest enemy in his young life, boredom.

But the challenge to the 4.10 had been different, he sensed as the sandy miles flowed beneath the palomino's hoofs. Today he wasn't just raising hell but diverting himself from something that was preying on his mind, something weighty that couldn't last. Rackage wouldn't allow it and right now would be planning his next move. The rider's jaw set hard. The commissioner would never quit on him and he was too proud to run.

Somehow he'd mostly managed to avoid killing as he threaded his reckless path through life. He'd done this again at Shaman's Canyon with Stocker.

But the specter of more killing lay ahead which was why Jesse McKidd raced trains and danced with pretty women in the middle of the day. It was his way of holding the specter of his uncertain future at bay. But how long could he go on doing that?

7

Angry Grow the Guns

The Winchester crashed and a uniformed figure tumbled from his mount to disappear behind the dune. Instantly the platoon returned fire and the shack shook and trembled beneath the fusillade raking it end to end.

'Hold!' bawled the officer, and the guns fell silent, the riddled shack shrouded in gunsmoke. 'McKidd! Toss out your shooter and show yourself!'

'I ain't McKidd, you purblind fool. I'm just a — '

The officer's gauntleted hand dropped and the rifles churned again. This was the only squad left in the field from the manhunt sent out by General Kirk in the wake of Stocker's recent failure. When they'd disturbed the man cutting up a steer on Triple K they'd pursued him here to Lone Butte where he'd made a stand. They had already suffered one man killed and one wounded. So they poured the deadly fire in with a will, continually firing and reloading until the dark figure slipped through a shattered rear window and legged it for the draw, triggering back at them over his shoulder.

Another trooper cried out and fell. This heller could really throw lead, as they knew McKidd could.

Somehow the running figure made it to the draw and his horse. But no farther, as the angry young officer broke away from the platoon to go galloping headlong across the knoll, firing his .44 at arm's length.

The hunted man stayed in the saddle for some twenty yards further before suddenly lurching sideways. He struck ground hard and bounced twice before coming to rest in a huge gopher hole, bloodied face to the sky as the triumphant rider loomed above him.

'Got you at last, McK . . . '

The officer broke off. He was staring down at a bearded stranger who was certainly not Jesse McKidd but a rustler known to the law back in Bright's City.

And this hardcase nobody had just cost them one trooper dead and two wounded!

Next day would see the young platoon commander stripped of his rank and the wounded troopers confined to the palace infirmary, yet without one official word regarding the incident at Lone Butte. The commissioner had troubles enough without admitting publicly to yet another failure that could only add fuel to the fires of discontent and failure that were beginning to eat away at the very basis of his administration.

Meantime, so far as anybody knew, Jesse McKidd and his pards continued to ride high, wide and handsome just about every place they damn well pleased.

★ ★ ★

The richly appointed coach rolling across the broad *placita* scattering chickens, pedestrians, tradespeople and bench warmers was attracting considerable attention. When the equipage finally halted before the palace gates to be challenged by nervous sentries before rolling on through, speculation was rife.

'What's the bettin' Rackage is bringing in another guntipper to replace big Stocker?' sneered one.

'Nah,' disagreed another. 'Iffen you ask me, it's more likely some big-wig from the territory capital, or mebbe even from Washington come to lay down the law and to warn Rackage to start winnin' or start packin' his bags. I mean Rackage made a real big thing out of Jesse's bust, but now after all this time he's just lookin' foolish. He took over here vowin' to clean up the county, not to make it a laughin' stock.'

'You're both of you wrong,' declaimed a third, sucking sagely on a bad-smelling pipe. 'I'll wager we'll find out that whoever just arrived turns out to be a mediator.'

'What the hell is that?' he was asked.

The sage drew his fuming pipe from between snaggled teeth. 'It'd have to be some smart operator, I figger, most likely a man with some experience negotiatin' treaties with the Apaches or such-like who's been sent in to patch up things 'twixt McKidd and the authorities afore the whole kerfuffle gits outta hand.'

'It's already that bad,' insisted the first man. 'It's bin that way ever since the whole danged county got its first whiff that the kid mighta been framed in the first place. That's where it all started to go wrong. And it just serves Rackage right that Jesse made his soldiers look so dumb, then set about carvin' up his world-beater gunfighter like he was some kind of tenth-rater out at Shaman — '

'Sure, and not a one of ye has any notion what he's talkin' about, you mouthy fools!' a thick brogue interrupted scornfully. 'Chade Stocker is still the finest gunhand in all this benighted pagan territory, to be sure.'

They turned to stare. Then glared. For the runty Irishman with the hard-hitter hat and drinker's nose was known to be Stocker's dogsbody and gofer. Moran had enjoyed some reflected glory when Stocker was walking tall in Bright's City, but not any longer. He'd been both bested then spared in the shoot out at Shaman's Canyon, the ultimate humiliation for a gunfighter, while his sidekick stood charged with having deserted his partner in his hour of crisis — unforgivable!

As a result, Irish Dave's status stood at around zero, his opinion on matters worth even less.

'I'd hush up about your pard iffen I stood in your yeller boots, Mick,' he was warned. 'What with one thing or another, folks are gettin' pretty fed up with the way the whole Jesse-agin'-the-commissioner thing is draggin' out. I reckon if you was even half smart you'd get your shot-up guntoter out of the doc's hospital and get gone afore someone takes it into their head to set your tail afire.'

'Ain't you heard?' jeered another. 'Stocker won't have nothin' to do with this bum no more. And who could blame the man?' The speaker jabbed his pipe stem at the Irishman. 'OK, loser — git.'

'But what of the horse, ye poor ignorant idjuts?'

The group stared uncomprehendingly. 'Huh?' said the pipe smoker. 'What horse are you talkin' about?'

At that, Moran's sorry wreck of a face brightened like an inner light had switched on.

'You have to ask, you poor ignorant savage?' he said incredulously. 'Why, Mister Stocker's golden palomino, of course. The champion! Can't you understand where the true tragedy lies here? It isn't Stocker. That big lummox has been shot more often than any of ye have had the pox. That ain't news. But that animal what's fallen into the hands of some beardless hobbledy-hoy who wouldn't know a thoroughbred from a plow horse? That's a tragedy.'

He paused, an expression of wonder crossing his stubbled face.

'For to be sure the creature doesn't so much run as flies on the wind, mane streamin' like spun gold, the tail of him a banner announcing to the world that this animal is equine royalty, bred to the purple — a galloping god of a horse . . . '

They backed away from him some, convinced he was loco. And perhaps that was indeed the case, for in his checkered lifetime, Irish Dave Moran had taken every fool risk in the book, had risked imprisonment and even death itself in his passion for fine horseflesh, a preoccupation rivalling Stocker's dedication to guns and women. It was an obsession which might yet turn the tide of south-west history before this saga of sand, Stocker

and wild Jesse McKidd would reach its
end.

* * *

He was a tired man at sundown.

Rackage slowly reached out to
replace his pen in the fine onyx holder,
a present from his young wife on their
third anniversary. He stared at nothing
for a long moment before placing
thumb and forefingers in the corners of
one of his tired eyes. Another day
of meetings, decisions, complaints,
supplicants and a mounting pile of
problems. It sometimes seemed that the
harder he worked the more things
appeared to pile up on him.

'Er . . . sir?'

He lowered his hand and stared up at
Clutterloe. 'No more of anything today,
mister.'

'No, sir. I've just had them clear the
main hall. But there is still the senator,
sir. He's been waiting six hours. Luckily
Mrs Rackage was on hand to entertain

him, otherwise he might have thrown a tantrum, I fear. And there's General Kirk as well. He is anxious to confer with you about — well, you know — what is he to do about McKidd now?'

Rackage eyed his aide in silence. Clutterloe was good at his job if a tad rude and heavy-handed with people at times. He knew how to handle people and get things done. Rackage suspected that during his earlier days as he'd climbed the ladder of success he wouldn't have had a thug like Clutterloe on his payroll, not even as a batman or a bootblack.

Just went to show how his career had seemed to falter and maybe even begin to slide backwards since he'd come to the territory, he supposed.

Starting out on his career climb his goals had been clear cut; county commissioner, then governor, then Washington. Well, he'd made the first goal, but would never get to make governor any place until he demonstrated he could run a lousy county!

And all because some lousy young gun punk had somehow proved capable of filling the vacuum created by the lack of a genuine opposition figurehead here, in so doing offering the gray masses someone to idealize and follow!

Why hadn't he killed the son of a bitch when he'd had the chance!

'Sir?'

'All right, damnit. Send the pox doctor in!'

'You mean the senator, commiss — ?'

'Get out, you moron!'

He was composed again by time the Washington man was ushered in by a pale Clutterloe. The man was portly, full of himself and serious, very serious.

Rackage knew why.

This political hack had spent recent weeks in the county watching and observing. Now he was forced to sit and listen while the man droned on about the situation in his province and how it was creating such deep concerns in the corridors of Federal power. Unrest, uncertainty about the future, talk of rebellion, unsavoury gossip . . . To listen to the man you'd think disaster was just round the corner.

Yet Rackage barely heard. Times like this he tended to revert to type. During his early days he'd ruthlessly refused to be intimidated by anything or anybody. He was still very much that ruthless man as he sat there with hooded eyelids imagining how good it would feel to toss this man into one of the city's sewerage tunnels then drop the lid on him.

He'd heard it all before: Was it true that Rackage's rival, Jacob Jacobs, was spreading rumours of the Rackages' personal involvement with the man McKidd? Or that there were ever increasing suspicions concerning the reason for the youth's incarceration and the actual shooting of the deputy itself?

The senator also demanded to know why the militia had failed so miserably in the outlaw's manhunt, a failure compounded in the public view by the Stocker matter which appeared to have whipped up pro and anti-administration sentiment to a point where, from Washington's viewpoint, it might appear that Rackage was now in danger of losing control.

Rackage parried, explained, soothed, reassured. But in the end the fat senator still demanded an answer to his most pressing question. Namely, exactly what plan of operations did the commissioner have in mind to improve the general situation in order to bring about the re-establishment of genuine law and order?

The best Rackage could do was ask for time. He ushered the Washington man out with the assurance that he would have his answer come morning.

Alone again over a glass of cognac as twilight tinged the skies above the Dragoon Mountains, Rackage feared he now knew what his solution must be.

Send his troopers back in again after McKidd.

He'd been reluctant to take that step up until now, aware of just how bad it would appear to employ forty or fifty men to catch just one stripling: swatting a mosquito with a sledgehammer.

And of course it didn't help any to reflect that the army, such as it was, had failed him before. As indeed his choice of Chade Stocker had already proven.

But he must take positive action now, yet he was still paradoxically reluctant. Bring in the troopers! Always bring in the militia when all else failed. Turn an incident into a war. Surely such a step was always viewed as an admission of failure.

He cursed and struck the desk with his fist. Ruthless by nature, his ruthlessness appeared to be failing him these days. Now he wanted to lash out, destroy and fill graves if that was what it took to regain the upper hand and dominate again as he'd done in his earlier days.

Muttering an imprecation, he rang the little silver desk-bell and Clutterloe's big head immediately appeared around the door.

'I'll see the goddamn colonel now!'

'Yes, sir!'

Kirk proved eager for the task. But even the man's eagerness somehow offended. For there were persistent rumours to the effect that Colonel Kirk and Jacob Jacobs might be plotting to team up and overthrow Rackage should the current instability continue.

Of course, it was part of Rackage's responsibility to detect and eradicate potential palace revolts, along with all the other myriad of duties he was expected to discharge.

Why was it the county commissioner was expected to handle everything, even treachery in his own ranks?

At such times he might be tempted to wonder if it was all worth it, knowing deep down that it was, every last lousy little bit of it.

The power, the fame, the next step upwards. It was a drug a man couldn't live without.

He sat half listening to the ramrod erect Kirk explain where mistakes had been made during the earlier manhunt and how he intended countering them now.

'That hellion must be run ragged by this, sir. Plainly he's either too fool-hardy or stupid to flee the county. He really should, as over time we've learned more and more about his connections and his likely hiding places. If, as you have just said, you will give me the full authority I didn't have before, I feel I could guarantee either his death or capture, say, within ten days.' The man paused, raising bushy brows. 'Er, is he still to be taken alive in order that the county will actually get to witness his trial and punishment, commissioner?'

Rackage was staring at the door beyond which his wife sat in the anteroom, waiting for him to be through.

He rose, went to the door and opened it.

'No, Colonel,' he said loudly. 'I've decided that this restriction could make things more difficult for you than they need be. I want McKidd dead and I want it soon. Is that plain enough for you?'

It was crystal clear to Colonel Kirk. As it also was to the pale-faced woman seated in a straight-backed chair, staring at her husband's face.

★   ★   ★

He didn't plan it to happen, it just did. One moment she was massaging his shoulders, the next she was slipping out of her clothes and joining him beneath the coverlet of the big brass bed.

Stocker was momentarily surprised. Customarily he was cast in the role of the hunter, not the hunted. Then came the uncertainty. Was he fit enough?

Treating the thought with the contempt it deserved, he ran his hands over her body. Marta trembled. She was warm and soft, just the way he liked.

The gunfighter smiled in the gloom as her naked body came against his own. He realized he'd been fooling himself, lolling about here thinking.

Jesse McKidd had really done him some damage with his lousy lucky shot. He'd about convinced himself he was going to take a week to recover, suddenly realized he was feeling like the fittest stud in this lousy county.

'Oh, Señor, you are so . . . so . . . '

'I know just what you mean.'

He caressed her silky hair and then her face was above his and he kissed her hungrily, feeling the life force returning in a rush. The next instant he was hurling her roughly aside as he rolled away and clawed at the gun hanging off of the bedpost.

'You won't need a gun, Mr Stocker.'

The voice was low, somehow familiar and very definitely feminine. Despite the gloom, Marta realized who it was first, and with a little squeal of embarrassment, snatched up her dress and vanished into the adjoining room, leaving Stocker now reaching for his vestas instead of the Colt.

The match flared hot and yellow to bathe the commissioner's wife in its quick light.

This was a test of the Stocker equanimity. He passed with flying colors as, swinging his legs to the floor, he stood as naked as the day God made him, lifted the chimney of the lamp and touched the wick into life with the tiny flame.

He blew out the match and reached for the smoke he'd rolled earlier, looming over her, the bronze of his flesh dark in contrast with the strapping that encased his lower ribcage and flank. To the woman's eyes, he appeared huge, swarthy and, despite the manifest signs of recent damage, indestructible.

'Feeling somewhat recovered arc we, Mr Stocker?'

'You can call me Chade,' he said, moving to the chair where his pants hung. 'What can I do for you, lady?'

Carrie Rackage dabbed quickly at her eyes as he turned his back. He was not meant to see, but he did. Weeping women didn't reach him. He believed they used tears as calculatingly as he did a Colt .45. Still, he did feel a twinge of something as he turned to her, buckling up the heavy shell belt and cinching the silver buckle. She was attired in dark clothing with a cowl half concealing her face. He moved to look out the corridor doorway which Marta had left half opened but it seemed the commissioner's lady was all alone.

'You must excuse me,' she said. 'I'm a little upset.'

'These are upsetting times. Take a seat and tell Uncle Chade all about it.'

'Please don't patronize me, Mister . . . I mean Chade.'

'Whatever you say,' he replied, lighting up. 'So, what's on your mind?'

She proceeded to acquaint him with recent developments at the palace. When she had left to come visit with him, the troopers had been readying for the trail on the parade ground with her husband and Kirk watching from the sweeping outdoor staircase that was an eye catching new feature of the old building. The full-scale hunt for McKidd was resuming and the orders were now to fetch him back dead.

Stocker gusted smoke at the lamp. He was amazed how good he felt. There he'd been, having medicos prodding and poking at him, swallowing foul gunk from brown bottles, taking chicken broth and going easy on the cigarettes, when all along all he'd really needed to boost him onto the road to a full recovery had been the never-fail curative effect of one warm body against another. It beat all the dope and tender care in the world; now he felt solid ready to slay dragons, chase after gun punks, even maybe help pretty women in distress.

Maybe.

Experience had taught him to be wary with beautiful high-class women, but he couldn't help but be curious. What did she want from him? They always wanted something.

He wasn't long finding out.

'Chade, things have changed. About Jesse McKidd, I mean. Denver had intended the men should take him alive, but has changed his mind. He's been warned he must clean up this matter swiftly and finally, no loose ends like trials or anything like that left trailing. I know he will see Jesse dead . . . unless, that is you can find him before that butcher Kirk does. If you could just locate him then persuade him . . . beg him on my behalf to leave the county while he still might. I know it's a terrible thing to ask, considering all you've been through, along with the fact that you were hired to hunt him down. But would you? I don't know another soul I could turn to who might have anything like your ability.'

'It's true, isn't it?'

'What?'

'What they say about you and McKidd.'

She rose from the crumpled bed, hands clasped before her, slender and dark in her somber clothing.

'Will you find him?'

'Sure. Meant to right along.'

She reached out and touched his forearm. 'No, I don't mean like that. Not go after him with a gun. I think I understand how bad it must be for you to have been defeated and hurt the way you were. But this is not a game, Chade, and pride and vanity don't enter into it. Jesse is a good man and all I want is that he should live, and you are the only man who can possibly give him that chance. And believe me, I know Jesse. After what happened, he will respect you. He'd listen to you as an equal where he would never listen to others. Will you . . . will you save his life, and mine?'

'Yours?'

'If he dies I'd die because the whole horrible mess is my fault.'

He might have pressed her to explain further but he didn't. He reckoned he knew all he needed to know, for now. Certainly enough to put on the trail again.

'OK,' was all he said.

'Does that mean you'll hunt for Jesse for your own prideful reasons or OK, you'll try and save him from my husband?'

'Guess I won't know that until I meet him again, will I?'

And the commissioner's wife had to be content with that.

8

The Silver Pistol

Drunky John had overdone it again even by his own excessive standards, and it was only when he was well and truly intoxicated that he felt reckless enough to dare go near a topic that had been disturbing his whiskey-fuelled dreams for some time now.

'I seen it,' he proclaimed to the regular crowd at the Two Bits Saloon. 'Nobody believes it, but I did. Plain as day it was, black surrey with the window shades drawn down . . . tall feller in a black cape with this big silver pistol, looked about a foot long, so it did . . . That was who gunned the deputy down that night. It weren't never McKidd, that's for sure. That kid wouldn't gun nobody 'less they made him . . . just like your outsized buddy,

Stocker or whatever his name is. You better believe it, Irish, on account it's nothin' but the gospel truth. Hey, Irish?'

The trouble with putting the hard stuff away by the gallon, a man could get so muddled he could imagine he was talking to someone when he wasn't.

Drunky realized he was all alone at the end of the dark bar. 'Hey, where's my little furrin buddy? Tom, weren't he here?'

'About an hour ago,' supplied the barkeep. 'You were snorin' when he left.'

'Liar! I can hold it good as any man.'

The man leaned closer, confidentially. 'It just could be that blarney artist is a whole heap smarter than you are, Drunky. All that bullcrap you've been spouting about McKidd whenever you get a skinfull these days. Don't you know that's risky talk? You're saying the law's lying about what happened to the deputy that night.'

The barman moved away leaving Drunky alone and looking confused. But he wasn't alone for long. The three men who emerged from the shadows all wore the gray of the County Militia. The thin, erect man sported an officer's chevrons.

'What'd I say?' Drunky was suddenly sobering and fearful. 'Did I say anythin' about the commissioner?'

'He's about the only one you didn't malign.'

'Thank God and Jesus for that.'

'But you said more than enough. What is it? Are you looking for a broken head, you whiskey-swilling slob?'

Drunky John showed sudden defiance.

'Hey, you don't scare me none, Wilkins. This is still a free country and any man who knows the truth is free to speak it any time he wants . . . hey, what you doin'?'

Strong hands seized him and were hustling him for the rear doors. He struggled but they boosted him out easily down the steps and into the moonlit yard where a storm of blows rained down upon the boozehound's sorry head. He gasped and staggered as they continued to sock it to him with short hard blows designed to hurt. Drunky had no defence and was soon down on all fours where the officer could get a good clear kick in with a highly polished calf boot.

Three rib-rattling kicks and Drunky John was on his back, barely conscious.

'Next time you start flappin' your lips, you pile of suet, you'll wind up next morning floating in the river face-down. You've been warned, booze-hound!'

It was a full half-hour before Drunky John could make it to his feet. He was bloodied, sick and sorry yet for some reason, still defiant. He needed some-one to confide in and being a man with mighty few friends, decided with an air of offended righteousness to go look for the newest of new pals, none of whom ever lasted long, that other loser, the one they called Irish Dave.

He was hurting plenty by the time he reached the livery where Moran housed his jackass, and where Stocker had stabled his beautiful palomino before McKidd shot him and took it from him.

'That Jesse,' he slurred affectionately, still at least halfway snickered as he stumbled into the half-dark of the stables. 'Sure, he might lift a man's cayuse as a kind of warnin', wouldn't deny that. But gun a man down in cold blood? Never. Cain't these idjusts see that . . . ? Hey, Moran! Where are you, old ugly-ass?'

He expected to find his short-time friend sleeping in the straw with his mule, but the stall was empty. Drunky John was suddenly so beat he curled up in the straw, not to awaken until the hostler awakened him at eight and kicked him out into the street. And still no sign of Irish Dave.

* * *

Hoofbeats echoed like Indian drums as the night slowly gave way to dawn, the first light picking out the figure of the slumped rider leaning low on the neck of a lathered gray horse.

Across the salt pans they rushed, scattering the small wild things that were up and about foraging early before the predators appeared to make the new day dangerous.

Presently the sycamores, which ringed the hollow where the little ranch stood, loomed directly ahead. Cutting down into the hollow the rider clattered past the white-painted outbuildings, startled the half-asleep milch-cow and set the dogs barking on the Double T.

The first figure to appear on the porch was not the rancher but the man as much on the lips of the entire county today as he'd been the night he busted out of the jailhouse in Bright's City's plaza almost a month earlier.

As always, Jesse McKidd was never short of places to lay his head. Also as before, the young man looked relaxed, easy and unworried as he stepped out into the morning yard to welcome Pete, not showing any concern until realizing his friend was wounded.

McKidd and his hosts soon had the young rider sitting up in the lamplit gallery sipping whiskey-laced coffee. While the rancher tended the man's flesh wound, Pete spilled the news.

'The troopers are out after you again, Jesse. They set out overnight, headin' for Mulrone. That's where I crossed trails with them. I had to know what they were about, but after they told me they were chasin' you again, they tried to hold me. I busted loose but got winged. But don't fret, pard, I made double damned sure they couldn't trail me. Not even that big bastard Stocker coulda done that, and like we say, he's about the best tracker we've seen. What ya gonna do, Jesse?'

McKidd made his slow way back onto the gallery to roll a smoke. The new day was well under way by this time, the sun climbing clean and golden out of the Dragoons to the east.

'Well, so much for them bastards runnin' out of steam after you cleaned up their big gun, eh, Jesse boy?' said the rancher, coming out to join him.

'I knew Rackage wouldn't quit on me, Buck.'

'Why? On account he's afeared you got too much support and loyalty from too many folks?'

McKidd studied his cigarette. 'That and a few other things . . . ' He sighed and stared east again. 'So, I guess this means I gotta do it, Buck.'

'Do what, boy?'

'Go face him.'

The rancher went white. 'You can't be serious, Jesse boy. They'll shoot you, hang you like a dog.'

'No other way. They're going to be roaming the desert and bothering decent folks just so long as I'm on the run. I gotta go to Bright's and call Rackage's bluff, tell the truth or this thing will go on forever.'

He turned to the older man. 'I'd like you to let them know, Buck. Give everyone fair warning. Will you do that for me?'

'Anything anytime, Jesse boy.'

That was part of trouble, McKidd mused when alone again. There were so many folks who'd do anything he asked, any time. He knew that if he called on the dozens and scores of old territorians who'd come to regard him as some kind of symbol of their own free youth, they'd drop whatever they were doing and ride with him. But that would never happen. He would confront Rackage and accuse the man to his face. If, after that, justice still did not prevail, then McKidd was determined to draw on all his resources and all his considerable power and influence to ensure that it did. It was the right thing to do, and regardless what his enemies might think or say about him, Jesse McKidd would always either do what was right, or do nothing at all.

He was the man the territory had made him.

★ ★ ★

He rode into the morning, the sun at his back climbing up over his shoulder, a big, wide-shouldered horseman sitting easy in the saddle of his rented dun soaking up the lonely beauty of the big land on his third day in the desert.

Stocker glanced back. He could still see it away back there on the rim of the horizon, just one tiny black speck of movement against all that yellow, rust and ochre.

He'd picked up a shadow yesterday somewhere in the Briarstone region and it had clung to him like a burr ever since.

He didn't much care who it might be, when it came right down to cases. He was hunting just one man, but didn't reckon trailing him would be McKidd's style. His style would be more like figuring out where you were going, circle around to meet up with you then give you the option of buckling under or shooting it out.

Stocker almost grinned. He felt like

he knew the kid that well now, maybe too well.

He was working on all the local knowledge he'd gleaned on McKidd as he swept the sandy regions now. Hunting a man, you got to know his habits, where and how he liked to make camp, who his close friends were, his patterns of running, resting, doubling back or holing up.

During the past forty-eight hours he had drifted in, unseen and unsuspected, upon a dozen McKidd haunts. He hadn't shown himself, wasn't looking for trouble, just checking then moving on.

Sooner or later he would strike pay dirt, and Stocker the hunter could be as patient at his trade as he was so often impatient and reckless socially.

Far away, like a smoky smudge against a deep blue sky, loomed the long line of the Dragoons. The capital now lay sixty miles off to the south-east. Stocker kept the twisting Lizard Creek off to his right. The land was rocky and solid here, but off to the north-west the desert resumed its dominance, stretching far out into the haze of no place.

He briefly studied the dried brush which led on to long, undulating dunes. He licked his lips to keep them from cracking. This was good for him, hardening him up again, putting the juice back into his joints. He flexed his fingers and wondered if McKidd would make it impossible not to kill him. If he was as much like the young Stocker had been at that age it might prove impossible to avoid gunsmoke.

He pushed his horse toward the horizon and the sun burned a hole in his back.

★   ★   ★

Stocker was making for the little hard-scrabble spread of Toland Tutt, the Double T.

Dusk found him squatting on his haunches in a stand of sycamores staring across an acre of open ground at his palomino.

The animal was in the horse yard eating from a battered tin trough. It appeared unharmed, looked to be in tiptop condition in truth. Sure, he was glad to see it, but he wasn't the kind to go overboard about anything much. There was just another nondescript saddle horse and a work mule to be seen in the yard. He'd first cut his horse's tracks ten miles out in the sand, was looking about now for signs of its rider.

His pulse was running a little quicker now. Odds were that Jesse McKidd had ridden the horse down here. Or had he?

The doubt couldn't be denied. He believed if McKidd were any place close, he'd feel it in his guts, sense the presence in his blood and trigger finger. He massaged the back of his neck but that feeling still didn't come. He doubted his man was here, but he was prepared to wait to be sure.

Eventually the lone rider came in

from the windy spaces through the sage. The man showed up just as a little wind lifted, blowing away from Stocker towards the headquarters. Straightaway the stallion caught his scent and began acting up. Tutt emerged and frowned in the direction of the horse but Stocker didn't show himself as, from higher along the rim, something moved among the sycamores then dropped from sight.

Stocker was patient as a hostile. He waited until full dark before making a move. A short time later found him on the far side of the hollow, padding along in a deep crouch with the cocked .45 in his fist, unblinking eyes probing the gloom.

Someone coughed and Stocker saw the silhouette standing facing the ranch house.

'Freeze or you're dead meat!' he growled, rising to full height.

'By the holy virgins of Dublin waters — don't be shootin' an innocent man in the prime of his life!'

Slowly he lowered the gun and stared

towards the Irishman with a bleak and hostile eye.

'You! I should have guessed. You've been camped on my trail for two days. Now I find my horse and I find you sniffing around like a dog on the scent. A man ought to — '

'Boyo, you're misreadin' everything you see, as usual. I'm the finest friend you have, and but for me you wouldn't be hearin' the news, now would you?'

Stocker crossed to the man and fixed him with a gunbarrel stare. Encountering his horse and this lousy Killarney horse-thieving son of a bitch at the same time was too much coincidence for him to swallow.

'Make it good, runt.'

Moran spread his hands. 'Big news from the capital. McKidd sent word to say he's comin' in to see the commissioner. The whole damned town is lathering in a frenzy of excitement, so it is. So all the time while you ride about looking for the boyo, maybe McKidd is already in Bright's City and you've missed him again.'

'Are you trying to tell me you rode all this way just to find me and tell me this?'

'Upon my mother's grave.'

'You wouldn't have got to figuring that sooner or later I'd find McKidd and that if you happened to be close by you might just get to sweep up the leavings and maybe get off with my horse, would you? C'mon, lie, it's the only damned thing you do worth a damn anyway.'

'Ahh, but it's a bitter, suspicious man you be, Mr Stocker. All I done was follow your sign down here, and when it got dark I wandered in, still looking for you. The blessed horse is just a bonus. I swear on my mother's dyin' breath.'

Stocker's head jerked round as a voice sounded from below.

'Who's up there? Would that be you, Stocker?'

Stocker didn't get to understand how Tutt had guessed so accurately until after the two had walked down through the early starlight to meet the rancher by the corral.

It eventuated that McKidd had brought the palomino to the spread in the belief that sooner or later Stocker would come searching here, not for the horse but for him. The animal acting up a short time before had convinced the rancher that the owner had to be somewhere close about.

'Why didn't McKidd sell him?' Stocker pondered, stroking the horse's silken muzzle. 'He's worth plenty.'

'Jesse's no horse thief,' came the firm reply. 'And he ain't no hired killer either. Not like you.'

Stocker just grunted and went off to collect the rented horse. He returned to transfer the saddle from one animal to the other. He could have debated morality with Tutt, but he had a long way to ride and fast. Jesse McKidd in Bright's City sounded like a recipe for mayhem to his ears, if someone touched the wrong button.

Moran wanted to ask the rancher

more about the palomino, but with a hard-jawed Stocker already heeling away, there was no time. The Irishman also left. Alone again, the rancher leaned upon his corral fence. What he now scented on the chill night air was the smell of death.

9

Death Walks the City

The word swept through the city like a Texas twister. It reached the grand homes of the rich and powerful and permeated the mean streets of the slum town where many a householder had little pictures of a smiling Jesse McKidd pinned to the walls above their mantels.

Jesse was back!

None seemed sure why, although most suspected he'd returned to clear his name, as he'd threatened to do.

Bright's City promptly battened down the hatches, those for McKidd praying he wouldn't die, his enemies taking great comfort from the fact they had Stocker and Kirk to back them up, until they remembered with a sense of shock that both men were out of town.

Had McKidd planned it that way, or was it simply luck running his way yet again?

It was possible this realization hit hardest in the big plush room where the commissioner was entertaining important guests. Of course, it was required of the head man to greet the news with a steely air of confidence. But later alone, Rackage found himself battling the clammy sensations of guilt and uncertainty. How could things have swung so dramatically against him so swiftly? Why did he find himself without his expensive hired gun and suddenly under seeming threat from a vicious gun punk?

His eyes changed color as the anger gripped.

He knew the reason.

Her!

Rackage moved to the doorway of the reception room to stare across at his wife, smiling at some pompous ass from Intelligence. Then she turned suddenly to sweep the room with a quick intense stare. Looking for her gunslinger lover, maybe?

He realized he was trembling. With a huge effort of will he pulled himself together. One man, he told himself severely. If he was going to allow one wet-behind-the-ears gun kid to threaten his power, then that proved what his enemies had long claimed — that he simply wasn't up to the job.

He summoned his adjutant and began issuing orders.

Several hours earlier, Jesse McKidd entered Bright's City in the deep of the night, a thin slice of moon riding the high skies and the stars too dim to shed light.

Sentries were abroad on the streets but they were few and bored. During his solitary ride across the desert McKidd had sighted Kirk's mounted patrols from time to time, always in the far distance and always heading the wrong way.

The capital was plainly way under strength. On McKidd's orders, rancher

Tutt had warned the city he was coming in. But who would believe it? Plainly the troopers weren't ready to accept he'd be that crazy.

He didn't feel crazy.

In truth, he felt almost fine. He simply wouldn't run and couldn't hide any longer. That only left coming back here and setting everything straight, or accepting the consequences should he fail.

And in this deep city night, walking light-footed over dust, cobblestones, bricked driveways and old planking, leading Tutt's loan horse and sucking on a readymade, he passed by the long high-walled alley which afforded a distant glimpse of the *placita* and a gaunt gallows standing tall.

He smiled grimly. They would never get him up on that thing. If he didn't get to clear himself he would go down shooting.

He encountered a bum on a street corner, squatting there with his hat extended in silent supplication, the patient beggar in the city with ambitions to become the cornerstone of the new modern territory.

McKidd paused to drop a coin into the hat. The 'blind' beggar raised his smoked glasses and gasped.

'Godamighty, it's you, Jesse boy! So it wasn't crazy, that rancher sayin' as how you was comin' in.' He seized McKidd urgently by the wrist. 'They wanna kill you, boy. But you ain't gonna let 'em, are you?'

'No chance, pal,' he murmured, moving on. 'Keep the faith.'

And wondered just what he'd meant by that. Faith in Jesse McKidd? What good might that do any man? He had no allegiance, no fresh political ideology nor concrete alternative to what the ruthless Rackage was dishing up to them. All he had was a vision of how it really should be, how men should live and how good life could be if folks just quit hating and killing and learned how to be brothers again.

'Sounds pretty airy-fairy, Jesse boy,'

he muttered soberly. Yet as he walked the old streets and alleyways of his childhood in this moon-stricken night, he suddenly felt an upsurge of new resolve that reached far beyond his original plan merely to come here, tell the truth and hope to clear his name.

That was too simple and way too selfish, he saw. He could wind up dead here leaving the corrupted system that had branded him killer and fugitive to live on after him. There were uncounted others to consider. Today it was him they hated but tomorrow it could be any other innocent man in his perilous position, a thousand. He couldn't let that happen.

But did he have the power to make change?

He halted by a ground lamp and dragged deep on his cigarette.

He was slick with a gun but would surely need a hell of a lot more than that to get any place. Then with a sudden jolt he realized with a kind of wonder that he already had that extra something. Popularity. Admiration. A following. People were naturally drawn to him, trusted him, showed ready to follow him. That was his real power ... and it had taken him twenty-one years to realize it!

He shook his head as he moved on. There was an excitement rising in him. It no longer worried him that he was alone walking the street of Rackage's city: the militia's city, even big Stocker's city if it came to that. But the night and the city were his friends tonight. He felt like a gambler clutching the winning dice in his fist — if he just knew how to roll them right.

He realized lights were still burning behind the windows of the Cable House on Mesquite Street.

He turned and went in.

The citizens gathered there greeted him boisterously and affectionately. As later did the upstairs drinkers above the Plank Bar on West, the late-night revellers at Mamie's cat house and the three-time losers he encountered on

Florian Avenue after stashing Tutt's horse at McCallister's barn.

And every man of them both excited and uneasy to see Jesse McKidd strolling about the city this way. What was he planning to do? Surely he realized the danger here? Did he want shelter, support, money? What could they do for him?

Standing alone in a shadowy doorway later, he knew the reason he'd not asked one damn thing of anyone of them was simply because he still didn't have a plan, only vaguely understood what he must do.

He was playing this hand blind, but at least knew who he could count on should lady luck run against him. The town clock was tolling two as the slender figure quit the doorway, only to confront immediately two burly shapes emerging from the shadows.

'B'Gawd, it *is* him!' a deputy hissed. 'Told you our watchers got it right, didn't I?'

They were slow fumbling for their

guns. But McKidd seemed faster than ever. His sixgun blurred into his fist and two vicious blows from his barrel saw two deputies stretched senseless in the dust at his feet.

Stepping nimbly over them he headed directly on to the plaza, where he halted. His blood was up, his time was at hand. Across the wide space, the old palace loomed high and dark save for one or two second floor lights.

Hers was one of them. The room of the commissioner's wife.

He remained there a long time unseen until the gate guard was changed, and that high soft light finally went out. He was long gone before a bloody headed deputy lurched drunkenly into the square to raise the cry that McKidd was in the town and raising hell.

★ ★ ★

Stocker shouldered through the batwings of the Two Bits Saloon and heard the big bar room fall silent as though somebody had thrown a switch.

In his younger days, to show up someplace and have people react this way warily, respectfully and, yes, shit-scared in essence, had given him a kick.

Not any longer.

He allowed the silence to hold for a long and telling time before his voice broke the stillness.

'Where is he?'

Everyone began gabbling at once. But they were just talking to relieve the tension. They claimed they didn't know where Jesse was, and he didn't bother wasting time trying to find out if they lied or not.

'Tell him I'm looking for him,' he announced and walked out.

Stocker combed the capital. He was sighted striding past the stage depot, flicking a speck of dust off his shirtfront. Loafing out front of Jerry's barbershop, squinting up at the sunlight bouncing off the palace's high windows.

He was seen on Back Street where a Mexican woman, seeing him pass, made the sign of the cross and clasped her baby to her breast. It seemed the commissioner's gunfighter was all over and with citizens lying low or deliberately keeping out of his path, it seemed at times that the man of the gun almost had Bright's City to himself.

While high above, the most powerful man in the county fingered back a drape and stared down with a smile. Even from a hundred yards' distance, Rackage could feel the power of the man's presence and was comforted, reassured and empowered. He'd not foreseen anything as dramatic as this hunt-and-hire drama between Stocker and the kid unfolding here, as if upon a giant stage, when he'd sent for his chosen gun. But it thrilled him and he knew that the drama would now play into the finale he had foreseen: Stocker triumphant, McKidd dead.

★   ★   ★

The city suddenly fell silent as though mesmerized. There in the fierce yellow sunlight blazing down before the commissioner's palace, and with the great man himself staring down, big Stocker appeared huge and invulnerable as he faced down Jesse McKidd, the boy from the wild places come to town to throw down the gauntlet at the feet of Denver Rackage, the man who'd hired the Stocker gun.

Newsmen drawn to Bright's City by recent events couldn't quite believe the primitive drama being enacted before their eyes. Even the trouble-hardened citizens of the southwest weren't quite sure whether they were watching some fictional stage-drama being played out for their amusement and excitement, or whether this really was the long anticipated decider between the kid and the commissioner's gunfighter, the devil take the loser.

'I'm taking you in, kid.' Stocker jerked his head at the palace. 'You broke the law and the law's bigger than

210

you or me. Hand over your gun.'

'You got it wrong, big man. Rackage framed me. He had me jugged on account he figured there was something going on between me and his wife. Then he set up a bogus escape and when I took the bait and hightailed it that night . . . ' He jerked his thumb at the city jail nearby. 'Deputy Murch was supposed to cut me down, only I was way too nimble for the man.' He paused to gesture. 'But the commissioner was across in Blue Rose Alley yonder, watching to see me die — that's how crazy jealous he was. When I gave Murch the slip, Rackage went loco. But the bastard was sure thinking on his feet when he charged out of the alley and blasted the deputy where he stood, then started hollering that I'd slaughtered the man and was on the run. That's the truth about that night. Rackage is a cold-blooded killer, and that's the kind of bastard you're ready to fight and die for, big man!'

Stocker was stunned by the other's

words, for suddenly into his mind leapt a crystal-clear recollection of some drunk slurring out an almost word-for-word account of that self-same incident. Yet he remained outwardly implacable and was still, as Rackage had once said, 'the chosen gun.' He'd come too far to reach this moment, expended too much sweat and blood, couldn't be side-tracked at the final hour.

'Tell it in court, kid. Give me your gun or use it!'

McKidd paled, his slender frame snapping taut as sudden rage flared from his eyes.

'I wouldn't turn over my gun to God Almighty, much less a has-been I've already whipped once, and done it easy. We both know that was just blind luck out at Shaman, Stocker. You're just a plough-walker and I'm the fastest ever — and we both of us know it. Mebbe you're too poisoned with pride to know how to back down, but you'd better learn in the next five seconds. That's all the time I'll give you to shift your ass and leave me to confront Rackage with the truth. One last hope you've got for walking away from here alive!'

A murmur swept through the ranks of the onlookers, then hushed again. A line had been drawn in the sand. Deep down Stocker felt he'd always known it must come to this. They'd faced twice with the guns, only to come out even. Now a remorseless destiny had stage-managed the deciding showdown.

He felt ready yet strangely reluctant: ready to prove himself the better man yet reluctant because McKidd had sown the seeds of doubt in his mind concerning his guilt.

But the code proclaimed them to be enemies. The scene was set before a huge crowd with everything hinging on the outcome. There was no way back for either man, only forward into the unknown.

The dense throng still appeared locked in unnatural silence as each man lowered his hand to gun level then stood motionless, poised on the brink of death or glory.

Then, 'Stop!'

It was a big voice roughened by whiskey and shaking with fear. Facing gunslingers and onlookers alike swung about to see the dishevelled, familiar bulk of Drunky John break away from the group gathered before the Civil War statue, the shambling figure not pausing until isolated in the wash of yellow sunlight flooding the center square now occupied only by two men with hands hovering over gun handles.

'Hear me!' the drunk shouted, and astonished onlookers realized that booze-addled Drunky John was actually standing erect, that he spoke without his customary slurring that, amazingly, he actually appeared alert and clear-eyed as none had never seen him. 'That's right!' he bawled defiantly. 'I'm sober today on account I had a hunch I might have to be before this day was out.' He cleared his throat and made a sweeping gesture. 'And sober as a priest and with God as my judge, I'm sayin' it's right what Jesse says on account I seen it all that night . . . seen them openin' the lockup door . . . Jesse nippin' off like a lightnin' bug and then . . . and then . . . Rackage lungin' outta the alley yonder and pumpin' three shots into poor Dave Murch like he was shootin' a rabid dog.'

He paused to dash away a tear in the hushed silence.

'I shoulda come forward before but I was too scared and — '

The sudden commotion from McCallister's barn across by the haberdashers shattered the tension like a rifle shot. There was a wild curse, the enraged scream of a horse, hammering of angry hoofs against timber planking followed by a half-fastened door giving way under the driving impact of the wild-eyed palomino that was dragging a howling figure bouncing at the end of a long rope through the dust.

'That horse-thieving Irish bum — !' Still primed for the showdown, Stocker was slow to react to the interruption. But the younger man was quicker. McKidd was already legging it after horse and thief as half a thousand people stared goggle-eyed in the glare of the greatest anti-climax the city had ever witnessed.

'You moron!' Stocker snarled, rushing forward now as the palomino dragged a howling Irish Dave into a market barrow that exploded under the impact. 'Leave go that rope and get the hell out of — '

He broke off abruptly. Moran had already managed to free himself from the rope and was rolling through the dust. Stocker whistled shrilly through his teeth to bring the animal to a sudden quivering halt some distance away. The kid stood scratching his head.

It was farcical now, almost funny. But not to Stocker, still mentally locked in on the interrupted gundown. Grim as death, he was heading across toward McKidd when through the dust rising above the false front of the general store on the south side of the square, he caught the glint of sunlight upon gun metal and sighted the hunched figure of a man in military blue lining up Jesse McKidd in his gunsights.

Freezing in his tracks, he caught movement in the corner of his eye and felt his throat go dry when he sighted more uniformed figures on horseback. Kirk was back!

There was no time to shout a warning. Stocker simply drew and fired. The roof-top sniper toppled over the false front and nosedived twenty feet into the street. Realizing the sudden danger, McKidd fanned gun hammer and cut loose as the troopers charged. In a handful of explosive seconds, McKidd, Stocker and a terrified Irish Dave Moran were hightailing for the nearest exit from the deadly square which just happened to be the gated archway leading into the palace grounds. Charging past the startled sentries with bullets screaming off the walls about them, the trio plunged headlong into the sanctuary to let loose immediately a hail of murderous gunfire into the startled sentries, covering the bug-eyed Irishman as he followed orders and slammed shut and cross-barred the heavy double gates behind them.

Pigeons panicked by the storm of guns briefly shadowed the sky.

10

One Man's Gun

Stocker smoothly raised his shotgun. The sound of boots hammering upwards upon the sweeping outside stairway to the upper floors drew closer. He waited then brought the barrel down on the head of the leading trooper as the man lunged into view. He buckled as though gut-shot and crashed onto his face. Without emotion the gunfighter seized the unconscious figure by an arm, hauled him across the walkway then dropped him over the edge. He fell twelve feet without a sound and struck the parade ground below with a sudden thud.

The others searched his face as he returned to the map room. It was blank and emotionless. That trooper would live, he knew. Which might be more than could be guaranteed for any or all of them.

*   *   *

The day seemed to take forever to die and even by then, no more than a score of people really understood what was going on behind the bullet-pocked walls of the commissioner's palace as twilight came streaking in from Nogales Desert.

The battle of Bright's City had been raging ever since Stocker and McKidd were joined by some fifty to sixty rebel supporters, but the compound itself had turned into no-man's land for the defenders when the big gates were finally brought down and squads of county militia and their civil supporters driven on furiously by General Kirk poured inside.

The commissioner had sustained a shoulder wound when the gates came down and in the confusion several daring defenders had managed to haul him inside the palace, whether that had been Rackage's intention or not.

It was only upon realizing that Rackage had been seized by the rebels that General Kirk and Jacob Jacobs suddenly realized luck had played their way, and reacted accordingly.

Amongst all the plotting and intrigue that had plagued the county in recent times, flint-hard Kirk and prescient Jacob Jacobs had remained partners working in unholy collusion, plotting the commissioner's downfall and looking for the opportunity to stage their own 'bloodless' coup, namely a strategic take-over from an increasingly unpopular leader.

The plotters might never have found the courage to take their grab for glory had it not been for the eruption of gunplay on the plaza that day, followed quickly by the startling realization that the commissioner had somehow wound up inside with the insurrectionists, automatically making him a legitimate target.

Quickly mustering their forces they'd

assaulted the palace in wave after wave under the pretence of continuing the hunt for McKidd and Stocker whereas in reality they were now even more committed to killing Rackage and ridding themselves of him once and for all.

Yet with dead men littering the square and medicos working overtime by lamplight on the ever-increasing number of wounded in improvised operating theatres around the fringes, the plotters were quickly made aware of just how formidable a task they had set themselves when, against all logic — or so it would seem — former enemies Stocker and McKidd had buried their differences to form a lethal sniper squad of two that had already cost them more than they could really afford to lose.

*   *   *

Driving a killing bullet between the shoulder blades of a trooper darting from one position to the other, Stocker reckoned he now understood exactly just what brand of treachery and pure evil they were up against tonight.

But for the moment the whys and wherefores seemed almost unimportant.

He was focused on just one thing as he snatched a fully loaded rifle from a perspiring servant girl and let fly at a dim, running shadow by the Capital Feed and Grain, namely, killing enough soldier blues to make the cost of their continuing the attack simply too high.

While down below beneath fogs of wisping gunsmoke where the noncombatants huddled, loyal staffers, servants, scared-stiff storekeepers and bar room bravados facing possible extinction were emotionally stripped naked as they let everything spill out — accusation, counter-accusation, allegation, denials, anger, outrage and a hysterical fear of violent death.

But the warring factions posed little threat to the cowering city. All each craved was simply victory and the sooner the better now. Stocker, McKidd, Clutterloe, Bourke and the half-dozen servants were methodically crosshatching the parade ground, gardens and surrounds below with whistling death between gun blasts. McKidd slowly began to realize they might be holding an ace up their sleeve.

It was when the lull came — as it came to every battleground in time — that a pale McKidd, a rifle slung over one shoulder and blood showing on his sleeve, lighted up a quirly and crossed to the figure lying on a palette in the shadows.

'Confession time, commissioner,' he stated loudly, kicking the end of the cot.

'Get this murderer away from me — ' a haggard Rackage began, but cut off sharply when McKidd hauled out his .45 and put it on full cock.

Grim-faced fighters watched in awe as McKidd accused Rackage of setting him up and framing him with murder. For a piece the commissioner heatedly denied it all, until she came forward. The wife. She had been awake when he'd left the night of the jailbreak, she revealed, as a silent Stocker and others gathered around. She was weeping for McKidd, the man who'd innocently befriended her in the loneliness of a loveless marriage to a man obsessed with his career. Tearfully then she accused her husband of murder and perversion of justice.

The big man snapped at last.

In sudden rage Rackage jumped erect and slapped her across the face. Faster than the eye could follow, McKidd pistol-whipped the man to the floor, was lunging over him in the moment a ricochet caromed off metal and slammed Clutterloe between the eyes, killing him where he stood.

'Liars!' Rackage raged, backing up and hauling a long silver pistol from inside his frock coat. 'Adulterers! No court in the west would believe such a flimsy tale concocted by a faithless wife and her pistolero lover — '

Stocker was fast, faster than he'd ever been. One lightning lunge carried him to Rackage to tear the weapon from his fist. He hefted it.

'Long silver pistol . . . ?' he said with sudden comprehension. 'Silver gun. Tall man in a black cape. Seems I've heard that description someplace . . . '

'From me is where you heard it,' the boozy voice of a wounded Drunky John chimed in.

'And from me.' With one arm about Carrie Rackage's shoulders, Jesse McKidd was suddenly as accusatory as a hanging judge. 'What we did was likely wrong, Rackage. But what you did was pure evil, and will surely see you hanged.'

'The testimony of a wanted killer and a harlot wife?' Rackage raged. 'You'll be laughed out of court and end up where you both richly deserve, in . . . in a . . . '

The angry voice faltered, the fierce light fading from the shaking man's eye. It was as if brutal reality had finally swept aside his rage and bombast, leaving him a suddenly broken man who was destined to play no further part in the palace battle. There were tears in his eyes, when the sound of invading boots was again heard thudding upon the outside staircase from below.

Stocker and McKidd looked up and locked glances before running shoulder to shoulder towards the sudden fresh outbreak of the guns.

Stocker blasted a husky climber off his feet, sending the man tumbling over the wrought iron railing of the staircase to plunge into the courtyard below

It was deadly shooting and with McKidd's gun smoking and thundering at his side as they formed the most unlikely partnership in Bright's City history, they were soon doing bloodily well.

But they couldn't halt the blue flood, not even when Jacob Jacobs went down under a fusillade when he recklessly joined the storming of the stairs. But bull-voiced Kirk was spurring his men on and in the company, obedience was still absolute.

It was when a defender lost his footing and spilled down several steps to within sight of the attackers that Stocker almost made a fatal slip. He went after the fellow to rescue him. A trooper concealed behind a balustrade suddenly showed himself and had his pistol levelled upon the gunman at point blank range when a small caliber .22 popped somewhere behind him. The trooper crashed dead with a sudden third eye in his forehead and Stocker whirled astonished to see Irish Dave standing above him clutching a smoking .22 in a trembling fist.

'Get down before they cut you down!' he roared, then hauled the shaking Irishman back to safety as, yet again, another assault commenced below.

The gunfighters continued to lead the defence fiercely but death was whispering ever closer when, through all the confusion and the screams of mortally wounded men, the deadly pair gradually grew aware of other distant sounds, a great uproar from the direction of the gates and the rising howl of many voices, which proved to be the preamble to the sudden storming break-in of two hundred angry citizens bearing arms.

The gunfighters knew they could not have held the attackers much longer. But luck had played its hand when they were driven ever higher up the blood-spattered balustrade by the sheer weight of numbers — until eventually the staircase battle became visible from the square.

For the crowds assembled down there beyond gun range could see for the very first time that it really was Stocker and McKidd up there battling the brutal bluecoats side by side, like compadres.

It was stunning, it was exhilarating, it proved overwhelming.

Suddenly ordinary citizens were out-raged and galvanized into action.

Emotion took control and touched off the stampede that flowed through the broken gates, across the body-littered courtyard and then went surging up the bloodied staircase after the troopers where, during an unforgettable span of murderous minutes, they were destined to carry the day onwards to triumph by sheer weight of numbers — while the capital's man in the street earned the mantle of hero.

The last gun smoked just as the gibbous moon slid behind the Dinosaurs to become a beam, a point of light, a speck of gold, then slipped from sight.

★ ★ ★

'Ahh, the top of the mornin' to you boyos.'

'Howdy do, Irish.'

'Never better, never better. Now which one of you fine fellers is goin' to treat a man — a fightin' man . . . to a drop of the doin's?'

'Get lost, you bum.'

'May every snake and viper, every evil reptile and venomous creature that crawls — such as the divine St Patrick drove out of old Ireland — descend upon you and your loved ones in the dark of night and send you to hell without the chance to be goin' to confession.'

None paid the slightest notice to the vicious curse, so Moran just sighed tragically and lowered his sorry bottom to the court-house steps and took out his breakfast.

'Where is the joy?' he lamented, spooning peach juice out of a can into his wide mouth. 'So the commissioner's gone to prison, the judges and juries have packed up and left. The ungrateful Stocker is the big hero and the senator from Washington walks the streets with Jesse McKidd now he is once again a free man.' He spread his hands. 'Yet, by the faith, it's still all so serious, like the funeral, you'd think we'd lost. Where is the fun? Who laughs?'

'Well, I'm laughin' for one,' confessed unlikely hero and new pal Drunky John, still respectable in the suit they'd provided for him at the trial, where his damning evidence on the deputy's murder had driven the final nail into the commissioner's coffin. 'For I'm a hero too now. Who'd have ever thought it?'

'It would seem everyone is a hero but meself,' Moran said tragically. 'But am I mistaken in thinkin' I fought the battle of the staircase as bravely as the next man? Did I dream that I saved fine Stocker's hide at great risk to me own . . . and he never so much as even said thank you. Did I dream all that?'

No response. Moran had been grouching and cadging drinks around town ever since the interim administration had been installed. He was beginning to get on folks' nerves.

'Must have done,' he went on. 'Just as I must have dreamed that, to rub salt into me wounds, that dirty pistoleer then disappears leavin' me to tend his palomino while he goes off tomcattin' or whatever gunfighters do between jobs. Talk about treatin' a man like dirt!'

It was silent for a time before Drunky John frowned and turned to stare intently at the Irishman.

'Is it true that he left you to look after that horse of his?'

'That he did.' He paused to spit drily. 'Then vanished.'

Drunky John's drink-ruined visage split into a grin. 'But wouldn't that be like leavin' a booze-hound to watch over a man's bottled supplies?'

Everybody laughed, for the Irishman's passion for fine horseflesh and his record for horse-thieving had been made public during the court hearings.

It was the last straw.

Red-faced and cursing bitterly, Moran got up and stomped away in battered boots and flapping pants. He was heading for a slum town diva he knew of where he might be able to cadge a shot, when he stopped as

233

abruptly as if hitting an invisible wall.

'Wait a minute . . . ' he breathed. 'Gone . . . left me to tend to the beauty . . . no sign of him in two days . . . ?' He banged the heel of his hand against his forehead with such vigor that he staggered. 'Moran, Moran, Moran! Where's the brain the good Lord gave you, man?'

★ ★ ★

It was just on dark when the liveryman from the stables on the plaza made his urgent way clear across the city to the last of the streets and the out-of-the-way rooming house hidden behind the planted pine grove.

He found the man he'd come looking for seated on the back porch sipping cold lemonade with the proprietor's daughter. Stocker now looked so relaxed and content in the aftermath of all the violence and upheaval that the liveryman felt almost reluctant to deliver the bad news. Yet it had to be done and he did it. He duly reported that Stocker's palomino had been stolen from under his nose, and that Irish Dave Moran had been seen leading the animal away at sunset.

He waited for the explosion. It didn't come. Stocker offered him lemonade.

'But . . . but you don't understand, Mr Stocker. That hoss . . . that drunken rogue . . . '

'I was beginning to think he'd never catch on to the idea,' Stocker said. He shrugged. 'He earned his reward and now he's got it. My life for a good horse. Sounds about right to me.'

The man was slow to catch on. Then he was astonished.

'Are you sayin' you set it up so . . . so he'd get to steal that beautiful animal. Are you crazy, man?'

Stocker didn't smile yet black eyes seemed to twinkle in the dusk light. Sure it would have been simpler just to give the man the horse. But the way he'd figured, if he was going to step out of character and do someone a kindness, he might as well do it right.

The palomino wouldn't mean half as much to Moran had it been a gift. But stealing the critter and believing he'd gotten away with it would be totally different.

Out there now, somewhere in the night with the golden mane flowing in his face like the wind, Irish Dave was racing away in guilty triumph, fearful yet exultant, a sensation of pure joy exalting his venal Tipperary heart.

*   *   *

Stocker rode along, the way he liked to. Stretching before him into infinity lay the wilderness, in his billfold the letter from the north offering danger and big money.

He welcomed the vast silences and had no fear of the solitude, for he had the companionship of the mind that complemented the heart of a gun-fighter.

What lay ahead was unknown. But

people always needed men like him who were shaped and tempered in the ways of these new lands.

He had crossed another border mark of his life in Canyon County. He rode on to face the next.

THE END

We do hope that you have enjoyed reading this large print book.

Did you know that all of our titles are available for purchase?

We publish a wide range of high quality large print books including:
Romances, Mysteries, Classics
General Fiction
Non Fiction and Westerns

Special interest titles available in large print are:
The Little Oxford Dictionary
Music Book, Song Book
Hymn Book, Service Book

Also available from us courtesy of Oxford University Press:
Young Readers' Dictionary
(large print edition)
Young Readers' Thesaurus
(large print edition)

For further information or a free brochure, please contact us at:
Ulverscroft Large Print Books Ltd.,
The Green, Bradgate Road, Anstey,
Leicester, LE7 7FU, England.
Tel: (00 44) **0116 236 4325**
Fax: (00 44) **0116 234 0205**

ROPE JUSTICE

Ben Coady

Dan Brady is resting at a creek
when, hearing a commotion on the
opposite side of the water, he
discovers a lynching in progress.
Brady's sense of justice spurs him to
prevent the lynching. But he finds
he's pitched himself into a bitter
feud. Now he is faced with a
powerful rancher as his enemy, a
crooked marshal, a bevy of hard
cases and a gunfighter . . . A veteran
of many tight spots, Brady might be
making his final stand.

GOLD OF THE BAR 10

Boyd Cassidy

Gene Adams and his riders of the Bar 10 had brought in a herd of steers and been paid. Deciding to visit friends, Adams, Tomahawk, Johnny Puma and Red Hawke retrace an old trail on their way back to Texas. But an outlaw gang trails them, interested in the gold in Adams' saddlebags. And ahead of them two killers have kidnapped Johnny's sweetheart, Nancy . . . Can these legendary riders survive the dangers looming on all sides?

DAKOTA GUNS

Mike Stall

Jack Thorn had become a hunter after some of Quantrill's Raiders, under Captain Charlie Chiles, had killed his wife and child. Now, with only Chiles left, Thorn was trailing him towards the Dakotas. Here the Sioux were squaring up to Custer, and Thorn's old commander, General Hipman, was defending Fort Burr. But Chiles had a new line selling guns to the Sioux . . . If only Jack could track Chiles down, he would prevent the greatest disaster the West might ever know.

REDMAN RANGE

David Bingley

When he rode towards New Mexico territory, Rusty Redman expected to find the Redmans of Redman City friendly to a man with the same surname. His outlook changed, however, when he found Laura Burke fleeing from her Redman kin, fearing for her life, and witnessed Redman hirelings bullying farmers. In Big Bend, he took up arms against their gunslingers and played a highly dangerous part in bringing law and order back to the ordinary people.